A Dangerous Time

IRINA SIMMONS

PREFACE

This first book in a trilogy is a tale of the early days of the drugs bazaars in Bangalore, India.

Beginning in 1928, it tells the story of three families, one very poor, one very rich, one displaced, and how their lives intersect in fateful and, at times, explosive ways.

Before Independence and Partition, India was a vast country made up of over five hundred princely states, all living under the British Raj. Traveling from one region to another was like going to a foreign land: different culture, different language, different foods, and different religion. The railway system was the only means of communication.

The fight for independence from the British had been brewing before the turn of the 20th century, and the day after it was gained, in 1947, the country was split into a Muslim Pakistan and a Hindu India. Massive numbers of refugees started to cross the newly created border to escape the extreme communal violence that ensued Partition.

Bangalore City, in the heart of the state of Karnataka, was under the rule of the Maharajah of Mysore, one of the wealthiest men in the world. When the book opens, he has already transformed what was once a sleepy village into a manufacturing hub, with cotton and flour mills, sandalwood and tobacco factories, and steel construction.

Rapid advances in technology and scientific discovery were changing the way people lived and worked, creating new opportunities for good but also new opportunities for greed, corruption, and manipulation.

At the dawn of what we today call the pharmaceutical industry, the old ways of gathering natural ingredients to make medicines started to be replaced by the manufacture of chemicals to make new drugs. Europe, Japan, and America began exporting these new wonders all over the world. Suddenly India was flooded with all kinds of drugs and cosmetics, using the ports and railways as conduits into far-flung cities and towns.

There was a lot of money to be made. It was a dangerous time.

PART I

SURESHA'S LUCKY DAY

CHAPTER 1

The Maharajah of Mysore was annoyed. His driver was ill, and he had been presented with a substitute whose looks he did not like. Despite being dressed in the usual smart uniform and cap, he looked dirty and untidy to the Maharajah. Who knows where they dug up this guy, he thought to himself, as he eyeballed the driver carefully. He started to say something to his stable master, but then just shrugged and got into the car. He was in a hurry to get to the council in Bangalore for an important meeting about the new hospital he was building. Surely they would have vetted this driver, even if he didn't look the part.

The Silver Ghost Rolls Royce moved out gently from the front of the palace. It was a lovely car, the Maharajah's favorite. The exterior was deep midnight blue, and the leather cushioned seats were burgundy. When he bought the car in 1911, it had been a closed-in saloon. A few years later, he had it modified to take the top off so that he could see the countryside much better as he drove through the Kingdom.

The only other change he made was to install a huge parasol on a rigid pole at the back bumper of the car. The umbrella had a red background, with blue and gold elephants stenciled on. Just like when his ancestors rode around on elephants with parasols mounted behind them to provide some shade.

• • •

Suresha Ravindran lived in Bangalore and worked as a porter for one of the biggest flower merchants in the city. He had to rise at one in the morning since the wholesale market opened at two and closed at seven a.m. He would meet up with several others, all pushing three-wheeled carts they kept in a nearby empty lot. They would all move together through the already bustling city, a convoy of twenty carts, talking, laughing, and joking. Once at the depot, they picked up bags of jasmine, marigold, and rose, piled their carts high, and headed for the newly built Russell Market. There, the gang would distribute the bags to various stalls just in time for the onslaught of customers. After the delivery, Suresha was always called on to do a few odd jobs for the boss, deliver something, move something, and by the time he was finished, around three in the afternoon, he was tired and ready to go home. His wife, Geetha, always had a meal prepared for him when he returned, usually rice, sambar, and a few ragi mudde, and he was asleep by eight o'clock, ready to do it all over again the next day.

Geetha was thirteen when she'd married in 1923. Her first son was born when she was fifteen, and the second one a year later. They all lived in a single room along with Suresha's mother and younger brother Girisha. Many years ago, someone had thrown up a single-story cement structure with a tin roof in an alley. As the city grew, the new families moving in would bury a couple of wooden poles into the ground on one side or the other of the hut, and anchor walls made of mud, fabric, or wood to the poles to make new rooms. Every year the row got longer and longer. Suresha had erected their own dwelling when they had left Mysore after his father died. Of course, when he built it, they were the last cell on the row, but many new ones had been added to the chain since then. The rooms were dark, and only one doorway offered ventilation and a way in and out. In the back of the strip was an open trench latrine, but everyone was oblivious to the smell of urine.

Geetha hated being pregnant. She was short, and her back hurt a lot when she was far along. She had a slim, nice figure, and was very vain. She took little comfort in caring for her children; she was just happy that she had delivered two boys. As far as she was concerned, her job was done. Now she routinely visited the special stall in the market where she would get the potions and plants to prevent any more babies. Her mother had told her about this, and she had carefully preserved the information in the back of her mind, knowing that it would come in handy one day. She took care not to advertise her activities, but she felt no guilt. They were so poor, she was doing everyone a favor by stemming the flow of babies.

From the day she was married, Geetha always shaved a few rupees off the allowance given to her for food. Her mother had advised her of this also. By the time her second son was born, she had enough money to go to the apothecary.

The little shop she had to visit was on the other side of the town. To make sure she was back before Suresha returned home, she rose early, before sunrise, to make some food for her sons to eat while she was away. She knew her mother-in-law wouldn't lift a finger to cook anything for them, so she got up quietly from her bed and moved to the mud chulha in the corner of the room. Geetha lit the bundle of twigs she had placed there the night before and didn't even notice the waft of smoke that rose from the flames and slowly filled the room. She pushed the twigs into the opening of the semi-circular block and placed her pot on top of the short chimney. She boiled water she had carried to her room the day before, and poured some millet into the pot to make a half dozen ragi mudde. The fumes eventually woke up her sons, both of whom cozied up to her, waiting for a handout.

"Amma, I am going to the market early today. I won't be back for a while, so you can feed the boys when they get hungry."

"Why are you going so early? You know I don't have the energy to run around after your sons. My back is aching, and my knees hurt."

"It's OK, I made some mudde earlier, so you can just give it to them. You don't have to cook anything."

Geetha rolled her eyes, got her shawl, wrapped it around her head, and set off. On the way, she passed many stalls and shops with lovely fabrics for saris, some showing bangles and ankle bracelets, and others offering sandals and slippers. Every few steps she stopped and looked, mesmerized by the colors and shapes. Geetha bought a strand of jasmine. She would pass the temple on her way, and often went inside to pray and ask for no more babies, the passing of her mother-in-law, and a better job for Suresha, in that order.

There was no permanent solution to the risk of getting pregnant. Suresha was a young man, and his appetite for sex was in the voracious stage. She visited the chemist almost every month, and worried constantly that she would not have enough money to keep up her interventions. Stealing the fractions from her allowance was tricky, and a few times she had missed her visit to the shop because she was short on cash.

Geetha was in a bad mood that afternoon. At her usual medicine shop that morning, she had learned that the old man had died, and his younger brother was taking over. He had asked for more money than usual for the Queen Anne Lace white flowers and seeds she always bought. After arguing and negotiating with him for a long time, she made some headway on lowering his price. She was angry that he was taking advantage of her. It would only get worse from here on. After serving Suresha his meal, she sat down and picked up her refrain from the night before.

"So, have you asked your boss about a raise?"

"I can't just go to him and ask for more money. He'll only tell me no."

"But we have a bigger family now. Your sons are growing, and they eat more between them than the rest of us in this house. Do you want them to grow up strong? I can't feed them enough on what you give me for food."

"Geetha, I'm tired of all this talk of money. You ask me about this every day when I come home from work. I'm doing the best I can."

"Maybe you should ask your brother to pay his share of the food. He is working and I know he has money."

"You know his boss pays him hardly anything. But I'll tell him he has to give me some money whenever he can."

"No, you tell him to give it to me so I can use it for food."

"Fine, and I'll see if I can give you some more as well," he sighed. He too was secretly squirreling money away from his meager pay. Suresha wanted to buy his own cart so that he could join the ranks of the merchants in the flower market. If he got a cart, he had a chance to negotiate for his purchases of the flowers, and perhaps sell them for higher prices. Maybe one day he could save enough money to pay for a stall in the market. But given what Geetha was now asking of him, he knew this was a very unlikely outcome.

He played with his sons for a little while after dinner before lying down on his bed, but he couldn't sleep. He was angry with Geetha for nagging him so much. But he knew she was right. Maybe he should ask for more money.

CHAPTER 2

The next morning, he got up determined to speak to his boss. Suresha worked for a fat old man who organized the porters. He was a mean one, always yelling and sometimes kicking his staff. While this was expected behavior, he had no idea what the old man might do if he asked for more money for his family.

When he finished his delivery of flowers to the market, Suresha reported back to the boss to see what other errands he had to do that day. He was waiting for an opportunity to be alone so he could corner the man.

Finally, he was called into the stall.

"You, what's your name again?"

"Suresha, I am Suresha."

"OK, yes, fine, you need to go to the pot traders market and tell Mr. Sangappa that we need thirty large clay pots for the flowers. Ask him when he can deliver this to us, and we pay the same price as last time."

"Sure, boss, but can I ask you something now?"

"What is it, what do you want?"

"Well, sir, you know I have two sons now who are growing, and maybe more on the way. Can you please give me a few more rupees for my family? You know I am working hard, and I do everything you ask me. Please sir, can you do this so my family can eat?"

"I don't care about your family. Send your mother and wife to break rocks on the road if you need more money. Now get out, go on, and get to Mr. Sangappa."

Suresha rocked his head from side to side as he left. He was not surprised but now he was worried. He didn't want to be labeled as a whiner. There were plenty of young men who would take his place at any time. He would have to be extra careful and punctual. He moved quickly through the streets on his errand.

It was a long way to reach Mr. Sangappa. He'd been to visit him only once since he started working for the flower merchant, but he remembered the location very well. It was the furthest he had ever traveled in the city since he had arrived there. He had to walk through all the different markets, cross the Mysore Road, then go through the train station to get to his destination.

He was excited to see the trains again. Even though his father had worked on the tracks in Mysore, Suresha had never actually seen them until that first time in Bangalore. He was mesmerized by the huge rods that moved up and down along the wheels, and he couldn't believe the amount of noise they made as they pulled in and out of the station.

Suresha went inside and climbed the stairway to the concourse that bridged all the platforms. He could see in the distance, across the station and past the race course, the government buildings and the British Cantonment. It was quite a sight. He watched for a long time, in awe of the grand, heavy buildings with flags flying from the tops. Suddenly he flinched and told himself to get back to work, or he would get into trouble with his boss. He turned quickly and pushed his way through the crowds, down the stairway, and out of the station.

As he hurried along the main road, he knew he had to cross at some point. This was a bit tricky, since it was very wide, many carts were being pulled by oxen, and some pushed along by porters. Cows and dogs were wandering around, and there were throngs of people. Suresha started to barrel his way through, anxious about the time he had wasted. The crowd seemed to get thicker as he moved across the road, almost making a barrier. He started to curse a bit and pushed the people in front of him to let him through. Suddenly, a gap opened up and he fell forward into the street. He saw something from the corner of his eye, almost on top of him. He was knocked off his feet, flew in the air a short distance, and fell hard onto the dirt road. He must have blacked out because he couldn't remember anything that happened in the ensuing minutes.

The crowd gathered around him and several men crouched down to see if he was still breathing. Someone said they should slap his face, that maybe he would come around. One of the men at his side called out that he thought he was alive. A uniformed man fought his way through until he got to Suresha's side. He sat him up and whacked his back a few times. Finally, Suresha coughed and opened his eyes.

"Watch out!" the Maharajah had called out to the driver. He had already chastised him twice for driving too fast, and now all these people who had not seen many cars before were all milling around, not understanding that he was trying to get to the council building on time. He told the driver to honk the horn so they would get out of the way, but it was a slow process. As the crowds lined up along the sides of the road to let the car through, the driver picked up some speed. Suresha, having pushed through the edge of the crowd with some momentum, had just come flying out into the road.

"What have you done, you stupid man?" the Maharajah shouted at the driver. "Get out and see if you killed him. What will people think?!"

The driver quickly descended the Rolls Royce and went to check.

"Hey, are you OK? Do you have pain anywhere?"

Suresha blinked at the man in the uniform, not quite understanding what was happening.

"Hi, yes, I am OK. Who are you?"

"I am the driver of the Maharajah. You ran into my car as I was driving down the road, you idiot."

"Oh, I didn't know, didn't see..."

The driver stood up and walked back to the Rolls.

"He is OK, your highness, he is OK. He was sitting and talking to me."

"You had better get him in the car and we'll take him to the hospital on the way. I don't want all these people to think their Maharajah is callous."

"Sir, I don't think that is necessary. He is just a common young man. He's fine."

"I will decide such things, not you. Do as I say." The Maharajah wasn't used to people talking back to him. This driver would never work for him again.

He slouched back and helped Suresha to his feet.

"Can you walk? You look fine to me."

"Yes, I think so."

But when he stood up, he couldn't put his weight on his right leg and started to fall. The driver held him up and slowly brought him to the car.

"You'd better behave. The man in the car is the Maharajah."

Suresha was still in a daze, so everything seemed a bit dreamlike, especially when he arrived at the side of the Rolls Royce and saw the large wheels with the chrome trim, the luxurious leather seats, and the massive parasol at the back.

Then he saw the prince in the back seat. He was standing up in the car, dressed in a beautiful silver and green brocade coat, and a matching turban with an enormous blue stone in the center, just above his forehead. The sun was shining at his back, and he had a bright yellow and green corona around him, the light reflecting off his polished silk clothing.

"Are you OK, young man? Can you talk to me, let me know you are breathing?"

Suresha didn't answer, as he was being manhandled by the driver, who was trying to lift him up into the front passenger seat of the car. Several men from the crowd had followed and were helping to push and hoist him into the vehicle.

The Maharajah called out to one of the men who had gathered around.

"Here, you, here, run to the council building ahead and tell them I will be delayed. I am taking this man to the hospital." He told the driver to give him a coin.

CHAPTER 3

The Maharajah decided to go to the British hospital in the Cantonment instead of the hospital for the poor. The driver shook his head from side to side but did not say a word in protest. He was sure this piece of dirt wasn't hurt at all, and he was annoyed that his boss was making such a fuss.

Suresha was still a bit fuzzy, but being a passenger in the Maharajah's car was dazzling. He couldn't take his eyes off the shiny dials and knobs on the dashboard and was starting to feel a bit of motion sickness as he watched people, cows, stalls, donkeys and carts go by at speed. Suddenly he remembered his errand to Mr. Sangappa and felt a pang. His boss was going to be very angry.

He leaned into the driver and whispered, "Where are we going?"

"Just be quiet. You will see."

"Can you take me to Mr. Sangappa's? I have to give him an order for my boss."

"Didn't you hear me? I told you to be quiet. You must do as you're told by the Maharajah."

Suresha opened his mouth to protest but changed his mind. He decided he had no business interfering in whatever was going to happen to him. He looked back at the Maharajah and smiled feebly.

When they arrived at the hospital, the Maharajah got down from the car and went inside. Suresha looked up in awe at the vision in front of him. He was amazed at the dimensions of the building. It was three stories high and had four elaborate roofs at each corner. An even larger tower stood in the center.

"What is this place?" he asked the driver.

"This is the English hospital. You are very lucky. The Maharajah is going to take you in there."

"But what is going to happen?"

"They are going to check to see if you broke any bones. You haven't, have you?"

"No, I don't think so."

"I told this to the Maharajah. He is wasting his time on you. But he won't listen to me."

"Well, I can tell him when he returns."

"You are stupid. You mustn't even speak to the Maharajah. You are just dirt, and he is a prince, a god. You have no business opening your mouth to him. You just do as he says."

They waited a long time until the Maharajah reappeared with an orderly pushing a wheelchair.

"Come on," he told the driver. "Get out and help this man get our friend out of the car."

The driver rolled his eyes, careful not to let the Maharajah see. He helped Suresha into the wheelchair.

"Now, you are going inside and the white doctor will look at you. I am going to the council building, but I will send my driver back to take you home later."

The Maharajah had taken stock of Suresha, in his bare feet, tattered clothes, and badly cut hair. This was one of those horrific poor in Bangalore. He thought with some pride of his efforts in Mysore to improve life for this group of people, but not yet so much in Bangalore. He was sure this man lived near an open sewer, had no running water, and could barely feed his family. As he drove off in his Rolls Royce, he made a mental note to spend more time on what was happening in Bangalore outside the British Cantonment.

Suresha was wheeled into the hospital and left in the entryway. The orderly told him to stay in the chair until someone came to get him.

As he waited, he looked around, taking in the incredibly high ceiling of the hallway, the fat columns on either side of the stairway, the enormous chandelier, and the glass in the tall windows. He couldn't believe that such things existed. He was dying to get up and walk around, but he had been told to stay in his seat, and so he did. It was starting to get dark outside when finally a young British nurse all dressed in white came to him.

"Well, what have we here? Have you been waiting long? Don't worry, we are going to take good care of you." The nurse spoke in a foreign language; he knew it must be English, but he didn't understand a word.

She took him down the long corridor opposite the entrance. It was so quiet, and there wasn't anyone around. It was nothing like the Indian hospitals he had seen. Some time ago he had taken his mother to the hospital for women and children near where they lived. She endlessly complained about her back until he'd finally agreed to take her. It was a small, one-story, two-room building with a guard outside. Depending on the severity of their ailment, the patients were sitting or lying on the ground in front of the hospital, some with members of their families in tow. No one was allowed inside until called for. They had waited almost the whole day to be seen by the nurse, who told them there was nothing wrong with his mother and they should go home.

They stopped in front of a door, and the nurse knocked.

"Come in," a voice said, again in English.

The nurse opened the door and pushed him in. The room was very large, many times the size of the one in which his family lived. The walls were lined with shelves full of books, and red velvet curtains hung from ceiling to floor, covering the tall windows. The doctor sat behind a massive wooden desk.

"Beatrice, can you go get Ravi? I don't think this young man speaks English, so we will need someone to translate."

"Yes, Doctor, right away."

The doctor stood and walked over to him. He leaned down and smiled. He lifted Suresha's left leg, flexed the knee, then lifted his right leg and did the same. He picked up each arm, feeling from the shoulder down to the wrists. He took out a flashlight, opened Suresha's eyes wide with his fingers, and looked into them. He opened his own mouth wide, and pointed to it, hoping that his patient would understand what he wanted him to do.

Suresha obediently opened his mouth, and the doctor peered around with his flashlight.

Beatrice returned with one of the gardeners.

"Oh, hi Ravi, yes, can you ask this gentleman if he has any trouble with his vision?"

"Yes, Doctor Sahib, yes."

Ravi translated for the doctor.

"No, my eyes are fine."

"Does he have any pain in his head, any ringing in his ears?"

"I can hear fine, no problem."

"Good, Ravi, that'll do, you can go now. Well, Beatrice, he is fine. No broken bones, no concussion, he can go home."

"But the Maharajah said we need to keep him here until he sends his driver back to collect him."

The doctor shrugged his shoulders.

"Well, he can't stay here. Just bring him outside and he can wait there."

"All right then, off we go," and she brought his wheelchair back to the front entrance. She helped him out of the chair, and out the front doorway. Suresha was a bit unsteady on his feet but caught his stride quickly, and walked out to the front courtyard. It was now dark, and he really needed to get to Mr. Sangappa. The Maharajah's promise to send his driver back for him was long since forgotten in all the excitement of the afternoon.

CHAPTER 4

Suresha was a long way from home, and he had no idea which way to go. He had never been this far out of the area where he lived. As he stepped out of the grounds of the hospital, he saw a wide road and to the right, he could see the walls of the old fort. He knew the fort; it marked the separation of the inner city, where he lived and worked, and the place where there were many rich people and temples. He was puzzled; he had been sure the hospital they had taken him to was inside the British Cantonment. He stood at the main entrance gate of the hospital. The road was full of people, carts, donkeys, and cows, and he also saw a few vehicles driving along with their bright headlights on. He was enthralled at the sight, watching as they drove towards each other on either side of the road, then passed and continued on.

He heard a loud noise and jumped. A vehicle was moving towards him and he had a flashback to his collision earlier that day. He recognized the Maharajah's car. It stopped at the side of the road, just a few feet from him.

"You, piece of dirt, come here." It was the Maharajah's driver, but he was alone in the car. "I thought we told you to wait in the hospital until I came back for you."

"They told me to get out so I started to go home. I have to get to Mr. Sangappa and back to my boss or I'll be in a lot of trouble."

"You are already in a lot of trouble. I am sure they were expecting you a long time ago."

"Well, can you point me in the direction of the train station? Mr. Sangappa's office is just the other side of it."

"Listen, you stupid man, you are nowhere near the station, and I'm not taking you there now. I will take you home. You can sort out your mess with your boss tomorrow."

Suresha shook his head from side to side.

"I'm driving you a little way until you let me know when you can find your way home. I am not going to bring this car into the filthy and narrow streets where you live."

Suresha got in the car for the second time that day. He smiled to himself as the driver pulled out into the road. He was sure he would never ride in a car like this again and was determined to enjoy it as much as possible. He started to wave at the people staring at them as they drove through the crowded streets. He soon began to recognize the surroundings but didn't say anything to the driver. He didn't want to get out of the car.

"What is the name of this automobile we are in?" he asked the driver, stalling for time.

"Hmm. It is called a Rolls Royce."

"Roseroyce?" Suresha repeated after him.

"Hey, don't you know where you are by now? I am not going to bring you much further."

"Yes, you can stop here, I will get out."

He started to get out of the car when the driver put his hand on his arm.

"The Maharajah told me to give this to you." He handed him a flat yellow silk purse.

"What is it?"

"How should I know, the Maharajah just told me to give it to you."

Suresha took the gift and got out of the car. He waited until the driver pulled away before he crossed the road and made his way home. The magic of the ride in the car was suddenly gone. Tomorrow, he thought to himself, I will have to go to see the boss. He is going to be very angry with me, and I may even lose my job.

When he finally arrived at his room, he saw Geetha sitting on the ground outside the doorway. Everything was quiet behind her.

"Where have you been? I made your food but everyone has gone to bed."

"Oh, I had a very busy day. First I was hit by the Maharajah's roseroyce, then they took me to the hospital for the rich people, then the roseroyce brought me home."

"Roseroyce?" Geetha asked. "What is that?"

"It is a beautiful car with shiny wheels that doesn't need to be pulled by a donkey or a cow. And the Maharajah was wearing a beautiful silk coat that was so brilliant in the sun. Oh, and the Maharajah gave me this gift." He handed the silk envelope to Geetha.

"It's very nice. I can take it with me to the market. But it's very small." Geetha unhooked the crocheted button from the buttonhole and opened the purse. Inside were several paper notes. She took them out and examined them.

Geetha caught her breath. "Look, it's money."

"It's not money. What are you saying? Let me have a look."

"Not out here. Let's go inside."

They had never seen such notes before. They were crisp, clean, and shiny, not crumpled and worn out like most of the one-rupee notes they were used to dealing with. There were ten of them, each with a picture of a man with a crown in the top corner, and other figures on it that they couldn't understand.

"Geetha, I don't know what this is. What are we going to do? Do you think it's a mistake? Maybe the notes were left in there by accident."

"Are you crazy? No, this is an apology to you from the Maharajah for running you over with his car."

He looked at her, bewildered by the words she was speaking.

"Do you really think so?"

"Yes, I am sure of it. You need to be careful who you show this to. We can only ask someone we trust to tell us how much this is."

He scratched his head. "Maybe Girisha will know?"

"Huh!" Geetha exclaimed. "Girisha has never seen so much money in his life. How would he know?"

"Maybe Amma would know?"

"I don't think so. Your mother is old and crazy, and she never deals with money."

"What about Bina?"

"Well, maybe Bina would know. She is at least educating herself. She can read, and she is always trying to convince me to send the boys to school."

Bina was Suresha's older sister. She lived far away in a fancy house, and had married quite well. Bina had caught the eye of one of the railroad bosses their father had worked for when she was just ten. The boss knew that her family was very poor, and there was no question of them being able to afford a dowry, so he paid her father a brideprice instead. Suresha would have to walk almost half the day to reach her. He was scared, not sure what to do.

"Well, maybe tomorrow I should go to see the boss and tell him what happened. Then I can see Bina once I have smoothed things over with him."

"If you go to him now, you know he will be angry and send you away. You will be wasting your time. We need to find out how much this is so we can decide what to do. Maybe it's enough for new clothes for the boys, or a Godrej cabinet with a lock, or even a cart, but we just don't know."

The mention of buying a cart caught his imagination. Suddenly, his long-held, impossible goal of having his own might be possible. Just maybe. He pondered on what Geetha said, looking at her quietly.

"You are right, Geetha. Let me go to sleep now, I am very tired. Then tomorrow, I will go and see Bina."

CHAPTER 5

That morning, Bina rose and did her usual chores. She had moved on to an iron stove for cooking instead of a mud chulha, and she made a few mudde and some rice before waking her children to get them ready for school. Her husband had already gone to work, as he, like Suresha, started his day very early. As usual, her mother-in-law was still in bed when she returned from walking her children to school. Bina gathered her books and papers and sat on the floor under the window. She always filled this time in the mornings with a few hours of reading and studying. Her husband had insisted she learn to read, and by now Bina could read and write English. She had just bought a couple of new books. One was called *Mother India*. She knew it was very controversial and kept it hidden from her husband and mother-in-law. The other was a pamphlet by Gandhiji, which was very complicated with many big words she could not understand. But she was working her way through both books slowly and deliberately.

Bina had seen Gandhi in person when he had come to Bangalore to recuperate his health. He had stayed in a guest house far to the north of the city but had organized a speech at a school to talk about his ideas to eliminate the caste system, particularly untouchability. She had gone to hear him with several other ladies from her neighborhood. He asked the women in attendance to support his cause with money. When the women complained that they had no money of their own, Gandhi urged them to contribute their personal property, which was mostly the jewelry given to them by their families at the time of their marriage. That day, hundreds of women took off the treasures they were wearing on their persons and threw them in the basket that was circulated. At the time of Bina's wedding, her mother had given her a gold-plated necklace which had been passed down to her from her mother. This was her only possession, the one and only item that she truly owned.

Bina was sure she could see an aura of light surrounding Gandhiji on the stage. She was very moved by his dream to end the many injustices against the lower castes. It made her think about the poverty that was often invisible to her, but was exactly how her brothers and mother lived, and how different it was to her life. She was swept up by the crowd's emotion and embrace of his vision for India. She fingered her necklace and debated whether to hand it into the collection. She hesitated, deciding that it was not time to part with it. On her way back home, she stopped in the temple to pray for the realization of his message, and that it would someday help her brothers to be less poor than they were now.

Finally, her mother-in-law appeared at the doorway of her room and demanded breakfast.

"But it is almost time for lunch, Amma!" Bina exclaimed, smiling. "You have slept a long time."

"Why did you let me sleep so much? You should have woken me."

"But when I wake you, you get mad at me! So I let you sleep."

"Well, what have you got to eat? I am very hungry."

"There are some ragi and some dhal in the kitchen, do you want me to bring them for you?"

"Yes, and some tea."

"Of course. Why don't you go to your room and I'll bring you a plate and your drink."

Her mother-in-law shuffled off back to her room. She was a very sour old woman and never had a kind word for anyone, not even her own son. Her grandchildren gave her a wide berth since she always complained that they were too noisy.

Bina felt sorry for her. She had a lot of aches and pains and walked with great difficulty. Her husband had taken her to the doctor, and he had given her some pills, but she claimed that they did absolutely nothing for her.

Bina started to get up to go to the kitchen when there was a knock on the door. She was surprised since they rarely had unexpected guests. She opened the front door and saw a small beggar child there.

"How did you get here?" she exclaimed. "Why did the gardener let you up here?" She grabbed the child by the arm and started down the stairs.

"Please, mam. Please. There is a man downstairs he sent me to bring you."

"What man? You are lying, you just want to get some scraps of food from me."

"No, mam, no, really, he is downstairs."

She dragged the child down the two flights of stairs to the entrance of the building. She was going to give the gardener hell for letting this dirty little beggar into their building.

When Bina arrived at the entryway, she saw the gardener and another man with their backs to her. As she started to shout at the gardener, they both turned around. When she recognized Suresha, her eyes opened wide and a big smile came over her. She let go of the child's arm and ran to him.

"Oh, my beautiful brother, I am dreaming, why are you here? You are looking very handsome, let me look at you." She took his face in her hands and gazed into his eyes. She was overjoyed.

Suresha gave the child the mango he had brought specifically for his errand to get Bina. He didn't want to risk being seen by her husband or mother-in-law.

"Bina, I am here to see you. I have something very important to show you. I need your help."

"Come, let's walk together. We can walk down the street and come back. Oh, I am so happy to see you, my brother." She wiped the tears from her eyes.

"Bina, listen. Yesterday I was doing an errand for my boss. I had to go a long way, and on the road there was a car, a roseroyce, but I didn't know what it was, and I bumped into it. And in the car was the Maharajah of Mysore, and they took me to the white man's hospital, and then the driver took me home in the roseroyce and gave me some money."

Bina was having trouble following Suresha's excited recounting of the events, but she nodded her head as they walked along.

"Bina, there are ten papers, and each one has a symbol on it. I don't know what it is, but you are the only one I trust so I came to show you." Geetha, always cautious, had urged

Suresha to take only one of the notes. He pulled it out from under his shirt. Bina could see it was a hundred rupee note, with the portrait of the English king in the upper corner.

"How many of these did he give you?"

"There are ten altogether."

"Suresha, this is a very big fortune for you. It is a thousand rupees, do you understand?"

"Is it enough to buy a cart?"

"Yes, yes, this money is much more than you can earn in a whole year. You were right to come to me. You should tell no one about this."

"Why do you think the Maharajah gave me this money?"

"I'm not sure. Maybe he felt guilty, maybe he didn't want you to make a fuss, maybe he felt sorry for you, but you will never be able to ask him, so don't spend too much time thinking on this."

"I have always wanted to buy a cart and maybe get a stall in the flower market. Do you think there is enough here to do that?"

"Yes, I think so, but you need to be careful. Everyone will try to rob you, so you must negotiate and not let anyone scare you. If they tell you five rupees for something, offer them one, and maybe you will get a fair price. Oh, my brother, I am so happy for you, this was a lucky day for you yesterday!"

They reached the end of the street. Bina's neighborhood was nothing like where Suresha lived. The streets had been carefully planned in a grid fashion, all straight lines and right corners. There was an underground sewer system, so there was no open latrine, and the streets were lined with trees and shrubs, like a garden in a palace. They turned back.

Suresha walked quietly at Bina's side. He was thinking, wondering what to do next. Bina took hold of his hand.

"You must talk to Geetha about this. She is clever, and she will help you."

He looked at his sister and nodded his head.

"She already knows, we opened the money together last night."

"Good, now stay here. I will bring you some food before you have to return home."

Bina went up the stairs to her flat. She checked on her mother-in-law and found her asleep in her room. She rolled her eyes and smiled. Good, she thought, she won't be looking for me for a little while. She went to her kitchen, made a lunchbox, and brought it back downstairs.

"Here, you can eat this now, you must be very hungry after your long journey. Let's sit on the doorstep of our building together."

Bina watched her brother as he dug into his lunch. His trousers were dusty and tattered at the bottoms. It was hard to tell what color his shirt was, it was so dirty. And he was barefoot.

"Wait here, I will be right back."

She brought him an old pair of her husband's sandals. "Here, try these on."

Suresha slipped his feet into the leather slippers. They were a bit big for him, but no matter. He was very pleased.

"Won't your husband be angry, Bina?"

"Don't worry about that. These are old and he won't notice they are gone," she laughed. "How are your beautiful sons? I haven't seen them for almost two years."

"They are very good, both are healthy, running around and making Geetha tired."

"Well, you and Geetha are blessed. Maybe if you put this money to good use, you can send those boys to school!"

"Yes, Geetha told me you said the same to her. I will make sure we follow your advice. And now I have to go. Thank you very much for the meal, Bina, it was good to see you." Suresha stood up.

Bina hugged her brother for a long time, crying again from the happiness she felt to see him, and sadness that he would soon be gone. As he turned from her and headed down the street, he walked with a funny gait, clearly trying to get used to his new footwear.

Bina stood and watched him until he turned the corner at the end of the road. She shook her head slowly and climbed the stairs back to her apartment. It would soon be time for her to collect her boys from school. She wondered when she might see her brother again, and what his situation would be.

PART II
UMESH

CHAPTER 6

By 1928, the Maharajah had laid over 230 miles of railways, built hydroelectric dams, opened hospitals, and established several universities. He had started leather tanning and sandalwood factories and opened the first state bank. And even though people were pouring into Bangalore for the work that he had created, the Maharajah desperately needed more. He also needed scientists and doctors to run the hospitals, engineers to build the infrastructure, and administrators to oversee his projects. It wasn't enough for the Maharajah to leave a legacy; he wanted to ensure the work he started would endure.

There were many bright children in his court. His favorites were his nephew Bahadur, and Umesh, the son of his most trusted advisor. They were both about twelve. He lavished attention on these two, providing them with the best teachers and tutors. Not only did they study Sanskrit and their own Kannada language, but were taught to read and write English by some of the most distinguished British civil servants. They were also instructed in both Indian and Western classical music. Umesh showed a great affinity for the arts and was learning to play the flute, violin, and piano.

That day, the Maharajah decided it was time for the children to see Bangalore. He was grooming them to take on important roles in his court, so it was vital for them to learn what lay beyond their city. They had made many trips around Mysore already, and the boys had seen steam trains, palaces and gardens, and the British barracks just outside the city. They had also been exposed to a wide variety of the poor, from those who had built shacks and tended a few crops, those who had got their hands on a few coconuts and were trying to sell them, and those who just slept by the side of the road in the dirt with no work and no way to buy food. But nothing had prepared them for what they would see in Bangalore.

The boys loved riding around in the Maharajah's car. They would sit in the back of the Rolls Royce Silver Ghost while the prince sat in the front, next to the driver. They always had to dress very formally whenever they left the palace grounds; it was essential to appear regal and splendid to the masses. The car had been packed with food and drink for the trip. The parasol at the back of the vehicle shaded the boys from the sun, but it was still a hot and dusty ride.

"Will there be many people there?" Umesh asked.

"Yes, I expect it will be very crowded."

"Are there more people in Bangalore than here in Mysore?"

"Yes," the Maharajah laughed. "Many, many more. You will be amazed."

The boys looked at each other, a little apprehensive about this revelation.

"I have arranged for us to have tea with the Viceroy. You will have a chance to practice your English, and you will meet some of the British women. It will be a new experience for you."

The boys giggled and squirmed in the back seat of the car.

Their first stop was the hydroelectric plant on the south side of the city. The car had to stop in front of the gate, and the Maharajah and the two boys were each carried on a litter by porters until they reached the top of the cliff overlooking the waterfall.

At the bottom of the chasm was a long building with red roof tiles. As they stepped closer to the edge, they could see the winch lift that carried workers down a steep track to the plant itself.

"Can we go down in the lift?" Umesh asked.

"No, this is not safe for you. Even though the British built this winch, it does not always work well. We have had a few accidents."

Umesh was disappointed. He could see the spray of the waterfall rising over the top of the building, and he was eager to get close and catch the mist on his clothes. The porters had just finished putting up a tent where lunch was laid out for the prince and his two charges.

"This plant makes electricity that travels to the gold mines not far from here. The electricity makes hauling the rocks out of the mine much quicker."

"The power plant is a very big building and so close to the edge of the waterfall. How did they build it?" his nephew asked.

"It took ten thousand workers and over ten years to build. But it is a great accomplishment. It may well be the first such plant in all of India. Maybe one day you will build another such place."

"I still wish we could go down in the winch. It looks like you can get close enough to the cliff to see the waterfall."

"Well, when we started the project, I laid the first stone. But I rode down there on a donkey. It was much easier and safer. Now there is only one way to get to the plant. The workers who live down there only use the winch to get food brought to them."

The boys looked at each other, not quite believing there were people down there who rarely left the plant.

"On our way to the British Cantonment, I will take you through the center of Bangalore. There you will see how crowded the city has become. You will see how the poor live."

As they drove towards the main market street, the sights were not so unfamiliar to the two children who had seen such market roads in Mysore. It wasn't until the driver turned into the roads behind the main street that their eyes grew wide at what they saw.

The alleys were narrow, with barely enough space for the car to pass. Many people were squatting and standing along the road, so close that the driver had to go very slowly to make sure he didn't hit anyone. He kept shouting to them to get out of the way. The structures on either side of the road were made of wood, mud, and cardboard. There were makeshift wooden ladders in front of some of the shacks, which led to small openings higher up on the structure. The roofs all appeared to be cloth or empty bags. There were ropes and cables lashing things together and clothes hanging everywhere. The row of rooms went on all along the road, as far as they could see.

"Wow, it stinks here!" Umesh exclaimed.

"Yes. The people who live here relieve themselves in a pit behind the dwellings. This is what makes the terrible smell. This open sewer causes cholera and dysentery. Many will die from these diseases."

"Can they take medicine?"

"Yes, but usually it is too expensive, and they cannot afford it, and even if they get the medicine, it is often too late."

Umesh and his friend watched silently as they drove through the slums.

"I am hoping that one day we can build a sewer and drainage system to help these people."

The boys didn't understand what that meant. They were contrasting in their heads the way they urinated and defecated in their palaces, in pots which were carried away by their servants.

"It's so quiet here, where is everyone?"

"Well, many people are at work or shopping on the market street. If you come here at night it will be much more crowded. But we won't be here. We are now going to the British Cantonment. There you will see very different buildings. That is where most of the British live in Bangalore."

The Maharajah was enamored with British science, engineering, and technology, but he had worked hard to instill a healthy skepticism and feelings of superiority in his two pupils.

"The British think they are so much better than us. But you will see, there is no one living in the Cantonment that has the same wealth as we have."

The buildings in the British Cantonment were heavyset and square, not ornate and open like the palaces the boys had grown up in. It seemed that every building had walls and gates around it. The windows were covered in glass, and all the openings on the ground level had enormous doors. The structures were far apart from one another and surrounded by lush gardens.

They stopped in front of a long building with a tall spire at the end.

"Do you see this cross at the top of this building? Well, this is a British temple where they pray to their god. It is called a church."

"Their temple is very plain. Our temples are much more beautiful," Umesh remarked.

"Yes, I think we love our gods much more than the British!"

Finally, they stopped in front of a white building with giant square columns.

"This is where we will have tea with my British colleagues. You can tell them all about your tutors and all the subjects you are learning. They will want to shake your right hand when you meet them."

The boys were apprehensive about the meeting, but the Maharajah put his arms around their shoulders and guided them into the dark, quiet entry hall.

They were met by a Sikh dressed in a blue uniform. They walked through the hallway to an adjacent room furnished with heavy wooden chairs with cushions, a few side tables with lamps on them, and a large leather divan. Despite the lamps, the room seemed very dark to the boys. Their British hosts were already gathered in this room when they entered.

"Ah, greetings my friends. I am so happy to see you all. Here, let me introduce to you my nephew, Krishnaraja Bahadur, who is my heir, and his friend Umesh. We have had a busy day touring around Bangalore and we are very tired and thirsty."

"Very good, we are so very pleased to meet these distinguished young men," said an old man with white hair, a white mustache, and a beard. He walked right up to the boys with his hand outstretched.

They were introduced to about a dozen men and three women. Names were mentioned but were so foreign sounding that neither of them could recall the one before the next one was offered.

"Please do come sit." One of the women gestured to the couch as the tea and a very British assortment of finger sandwiches was served.

"So tell me, what are your favorite subjects in your lessons?"

The boys answered in short sentences. They were a little bit shy, surrounded by all these strangers. And while their English was impeccable, they were not used to speaking it outside of their classroom. The Maharajah kept jumping in to help them out.

"They are studying mathematics, algebra, geometry, biology and chemistry. They are both excellent pupils."

"We also study music and playing instruments. Every day we practice and play for our family." Umesh was starting to loosen up a bit.

"Well yes indeed, music tames the heart of the savage beast!" exclaimed one of the older ladies.

The Maharajah smiled at this remark.

"Yes, madam, we have a very long history of traditional music in Mysore. It is considered an art of the gods and has survived in its purest form from even before your Jesus Christ."

There was a round of nervous laughter from their hosts. The Maharajah was amused his point had been made to these British who thought themselves so superior. He was very pleased with how this day had turned out.

CHAPTER 7

Vijay Patel, the Maharajah's cousin, had asked for an audience. They had not seen each other for many years. He had returned to India in 1930 from the United States, where he studied Chemistry and Microbiology at Cornell University and the Massachusetts Institute of Technology. He was now developing various new curricula at the first private university in India at Varanasi, and he desperately needed students. He was traveling around India, meeting with various princes and wealthy families, trying to get commitments for sons and even daughters to come to his school.

"Your Highness, thank you very much for seeing me. It is a great honor."

"Of course, my cousin. You do me the honor. I have been hearing and reading about your exploits at the new university. You are doing our country a great patriotic service."

"Thank you, thank you. This is why I am here, Your Highness, to discuss with you the programs we have established, many in the traditional fields like medicine, engineering, chemistry, and biology, but also new branches like chemical engineering, pharmaceutical chemistry, and microbiology."

"Tell me what the purpose is of some of these new academic programs."

"Well, for example, microbiology is very relevant to the study of many of the diseases that plague our country. Also, the study of chemistry as it relates to medications is very important for us in India. I am sure you are familiar with the invasion that we have in India today from German, American, and Japanese drugs, all selling for much less than British ones. This has created some serious questions around the quality and effectiveness of these drugs."

"Yes, yes, I know about this problem. Only last month over one hundred people died in Bangalore from cholera. We discovered that the pills they were given from the hospital were made of chalk, not quinine as they should have been. The hospital told us they obtained the pills from the bazaar, the same as they get their bandages and other supplies. I was very angry, but there was nothing I could do."

"But there are things we can and must do to prevent this type of thing from happening. I am looking for students, my friend. There are so many intelligent, well-educated young men, and even women, in India today. Their secondary education has been exemplary. I need your help to channel some of this talent to further their education in the interest of our country."

The Maharajah sat back and considered what he was hearing. Convincing Indian royalty to send promising students into non-traditional disciplines would be challenging. Not everyone was like his friend, motivated by patriotic zeal to drive change. But he also liked the idea of being seen as forward-looking.

"I can also tell you that we will name you Chancellor for the next two years if you can provide us with a dozen or so students."

"Chancellor?"

"Yes, this is an honorary title that will put your name in the history of the university forever. Of course, you don't have to worry; the Vice Chancellor will manage the day-to-day activities."

"Well then, I can promise you that I will send my nephew and his friend, my ward, to Varanasi to study in your new programs. I will also tell my ministers and other advisors to bring another ten names for you."

"Your Highness, this will be a tremendous legacy for you. I am very grateful for your commitment to the advancement of our country. Even Gandhiji has helped us to find many new students."

• • •

A few years later, when Umesh was nineteen, he traveled by train to Varanasi to begin his studies at the university. He had been told he would be the very first student in the brand-new pharmacy degree program, and the Maharajah seemed very proud of this fact. His nephew would start the following year due to some royal duties he had to complete.

The journey took three days. Umesh was alone in the special carriage the Maharajah had made available to him. He read and looked out the window, but mostly he contemplated how different his life would be for the next few years. He had heard that Varanasi would be very cold in the winter months, unlike the constant heat in Mysore. He wasn't looking forward to that. But the prospect of being on his own, away from the carefully and meticulously planned life of the palace, had a lot of appeal. He wondered if he would have the freedom to wander the city, to maybe see some films and perhaps meet some musicians and writers. He also felt sure that he could find all the English language books that he wanted to read, many of which would be frowned upon by his old tutors.

A few days after settling into his apartment, he found several of his fellow students gathered in the main hallway of the residence. The room was furnished with divans, comfortable chairs, and an English-style fireplace. Everyone was sipping sherry from elegant crystal glasses.

"Ah, Umesh, have you unpacked all your cases?" He couldn't remember this person's name, even though they had met on the day of his arrival. He was older and had come to Varanasi from Chennai.

"Gajanan is my name, remember?" He smiled, recognizing Umesh's slight embarrassment. "Do you want a drink? We are pouring excellent sherry. Here, let me introduce some of the others." He took Umesh by the elbow and brought him into the group.

"First, we have here some real royals," he said, winking. Everyone laughed.

"This is Siddeshwar. He is the son of the Maharajah of Kashi, and this one is Madhavan, he is from Chennai, like me. They say he is the Maharajah's nephew, but we all know he's the Maharajah's illegitimate son!"

"Wait a minute, what about you? Who is vouching for your parentage?" someone exclaimed.

"You'll never know the truth!" Gajanan retorted with a roll of his eyes and everyone laughed again.

"Next we have the auspicious sons of the various diwans and their extended families." He went on to introduce the others in the correct pecking order, from most royal down to the lower rungs of the social order in the room.

"We are all going to the Aarti tonight on the river bank. If you have never been to Varanasi before, you have to come with us. It is an experience not to be missed."

Umesh had heard about the night ceremony along the Ganges. While he usually hated being in the crowds, he thought he should go out with his new friends.

The group left the residence around six pm. Three cars were waiting for them outside. Umesh was very impressed with the lovely pale green Minerva.

"Do you have a car here in Varanasi?" Gajanan asked. "If not, you should think about getting one. Walking around or taking a rickshaw is not a good idea in this town."

"No, I don't have a car. My father had a Sunbeam in Mysore, and I used to ride around in the Maharajah's Silver Ghost all the time."

"Well, I'm told you can get a nice Sunbeam or DeSoto, both of which are available right now. I will let them know if you are interested."

"Yes, I think it's a good idea. Thanks."

The young men piled into the vehicles and drove towards the Ganges. Their destination was a small but ornate boathouse some distance up the river. As they entered the courtyard, Umesh saw the barge. It was like a bejeweled floating crown. The bottom level was the largest, with columns and gold brocade ropes hanging along the railing. The second level was a balcony with linen-covered tables and chairs. The third level was a canopied deck where a group of musicians was just starting to play as they left the cars and stepped onto the boat. He had never seen anything like this before.

Once on board, cigars and whiskies were served, and eventually, the boat slid out from its dock. Umesh wandered up to the top deck, where he could see in the distance all the fires and candles floating on the river.

"Nothing has prepared you for what you will see tonight." Siddeshwar had come up behind him. "I grew up in this city and have been to Delhi and Calcutta, and yet this ceremony still affects me."

"We have a lot of lakes and ponds in Mysore, but nothing so big as this river."

"Well, yes, the Ganges is very big. But if you ever get a chance, you should travel to the coast, either East or West, to see the sea. It will make such an impression on you."

The boat was getting closer to the hub, where the ceremony was about to start.

"Oh, and once the ceremony is over, we will continue down the river a bit before turning back. There are a few ladies in cubicles on the bottom level of the boat. You should make sure you visit them before the trip is finished. I guarantee they are some of the very best in town."

Umesh had been with such women in the past. In Mysore, before he left, the Maharajah had arranged for him to visit a special palace with the courtesans. "It's to make sure you have this knowledge before you travel away from home," he had said. Umesh remembered how awkward he felt the first time he was in a room alone with a naked girl.

As they approached the area where the ceremony would take place, his eyes focused on the sea of people on the stone ghats that lined the river. Music from the banks floated across to the barge. He watched as several young men dressed in golden robes and scarves arranged themselves underneath a tall arcade with brocade parasols set at the tops. They blew conch shells to signal the start. The men then traded the horns for lanterns of gold with large fires pouring out of the open tops. They chanted as they lifted them above their heads and circled them around. Eventually, the lanterns were replaced by conical-shaped diyas lit up on their multiple levels. Finally, they swung incense burners and waved the smoke around so it would waft onto the crowd.

Mellowed by the whiskey, Umesh gazed through the smoky air to the figures moving around on the stage. He could hear the sound of the crowd gently over the music, punctuated by the ringing of hand-held bells. As the boat started to move after the end of the action, he thought he'd better get downstairs and claim his turn with the women. After all, he thought, if this was to be his new life, he'd better get used to it.

CHAPTER 8

By 1939, Umesh was getting ready to finish his studies and get his qualification in pharmacy. His life in Varanasi was full of parties, plays, and concerts. In the time he was at the university, the number of students had grown a lot, and he met people from all over India, including quite a few women studying also.

The Maharajah's nephew never made it to Varanasi. Umesh had only returned home once in the three years since he left Mysore, and that was to marry the young girl who had been chosen for him. But he'd left his new wife behind and rushed back to Varanasi to continue his degree. He had a good excuse; he was contributing to the advancement of his country.

But his interest in his studies had been marginal. The only reason he had stuck with it was because of the Maharajah and his financial support. No one expected him to be a great student. At least he obliged his professors by showing up occasionally and being polite.

In those days there was a lot of talk of politics, the war in Europe, and independence. This interested him somewhat more, but his participation was shallow. He did not embrace the debates with the same passion as some of his fellow students. He felt no obligation from his status, wealth, or education to change the world. He felt quite convinced that the masses in India would never come out of their slums and ignorance, no matter what the intelligentsia did, and that the British weren't as bad as everyone made out.

"The Maharajah has asked that you travel to Delhi to participate in the commission that is working to write new rules and regulations for the drug trade. They have been working on this for almost ten years. They need the contribution of people like you who are qualified in pharmacy." It was the third time Professor Patel had told him about the plan, but each time Umesh had expressed reluctance to go.

"If they have been working on it for ten years, then surely they must be almost finished with this. What can I add?"

"They need a professional approach. You can help them because you will bring legitimacy to this effort."

Umesh was skeptical but eventually gave in. He didn't want to return to Mysore to settle into domestic life with a wife he hardly knew. And he couldn't stay on in Varanasi, as the Maharajah would be angry with him for disobeying his request.

Umesh got to Delhi and hated it immediately. Shortly after his arrival, before he even attended a single meeting of the commission, the Drugs Act was passed by the Parliament. His assignment was to start working on the enforcement and inspection regulations set out in the documents. He spent his days converting the Act's somewhat bewildering text into standards and rules, mostly by creating hundreds of different application forms to obtain authorization for the importation, manufacture, dispensing, selling, and distribution of drugs. There was even a form that permitted the selling of drugs from a cart. He wondered how the commission intended to enforce these rules all over India. He had a hard time seeing how every single bazaar trader who got their hands on a few quinine pills was going to be forced to pay for a piece of paper permitting him to do what he'd been doing for the last twenty years. To him, it seemed a colossal waste of time.

He met a lot of academics and administrators who were not from the highest classes. There were also many more Muslims in Delhi, which was very different from the places he'd lived so far. The contrast to the calm and order he had grown up in was very sharp. Even Varanasi, which was much more lively than Mysore, seemed serene compared to Delhi. The place was like a tinderbox. Each time there was a festival or gathering, things always deteriorated into riots and fighting. Gandhi kept creating opportunities for the lower classes to march and strike, the Congress party was fraught with internal squabbling, and the fascists were emboldened by the war and the success of Nazi Germany. Every party and social event he attended seemed to veer away from normal and enlightened conversations about literature, poetry, and music into a debate about social injustice, independence, and self-determination. The final straw arrived with news of the Maharajah's death. There was nothing to keep him in Delhi now.

Umesh packed up his belongings. He had long since cast aside his silk embroidered tunics and turbans for western clothes and had purchased a wardrobe of beautifully handmade suits and shoes. He had accumulated a substantial library of English books, many of which he had read only the first few pages. He decided to take the long way home and traveled by train south from Delhi, first visiting the Taj Mahal, then Jaipur, Ahmadabad, and then on to Mumbai. But he no longer had the luxury of a private rail car and had to ride alongside others in the first-class carriage.

The day he arrived in Mumbai he had great difficulty finding a porter. A big Muslim rally was going on in the Bhindi bazaar, and most of the porters were there. The Untouchables had also gathered there since Ambedkar had decided to join the rally. It was a name he was familiar with. While at Varanasi, Umesh had started to read his pamphlet about abolishing the caste system but had never managed to finish it. Later he found out that the rally was meant to be a celebration organized by Jinnah and Ambedkar of the mass resignation of the Congress Party earlier that year. He wondered if this place was going to be just like Delhi, where protests and rallies flared up every single day of the week.

He originally planned to stay for just a few weeks to see the sea and take in some of the Portuguese history of the city, just as his friends in Varanasi had suggested. The city had a different personality from Delhi. It was smaller and more cozy, with a much more cosmopolitan feel. One could see many Europeans, Americans, and even a few Chinese on the streets, in the cafes and restaurants. Umesh took a temporary apartment in a beautiful green and yellow art deco building set at the center of a large park called the Maidan Oval. You could never find such architecture in Delhi. He spent many days walking through the town, sitting along Marine Road, watching the huge ships coming and going from the port. The barges on the Ganges were miniature by comparison. He saw many British warships, and for the first time, the war that seemed so far away was suddenly at his doorstep.

Umesh had come to the movie capital of India. Within a few weeks of his arrival, he was introduced into the film industry's social circles. He met movie stars, writers, producers, and musicians. With the war raging in Europe, these people also talked about politics but seemed much more relaxed about it. Politics was an intellectual debate for them, not a life and death subject as it had seemed in Delhi. While he mingled with many Congress party advocates, there were also many communists, as well as fascists who were very anti-British and pro-Germany and Japan.

"Umesh, here, I want to introduce you to someone." Rajiv was a producer and writer. Every week he held an all-night party at his apartment.

"This is Noor. She is the daughter of the director Jehan. She has just returned from Cambridge."

He stood from his seat on the plush couch. He saw a small woman with dark, almond-shaped eyes, a sharp nose, and a full mouth. She wore European-style clothing and looked right into his eyes as she smiled.

"Rajiv tells me you just got here from Delhi?"

"Yes, I got out of there as quickly as I could."

"I've never been there. I grew up here and spent the last three years at Cambridge in England. My father sent for me to come back. The war and the bombing have stepped up there."

"You are very lucky. Many people are dying in England."

"My father was tipped off by some of the All India people about the start of the serious bombing in England. I got out just in time."

"What were you studying at Cambridge?"

"Law, but I have to decide whether to continue my studies here in India. I'm just not sure if I am interested enough," she laughed.

"Well, I am sure you don't have to rush to make a decision, especially if you just got back."

"What about you? What are you doing here?"

"Drifting, sort of. I was in Varanasi for the last three years at the university."

"Varanasi is a beautiful city. I was there as a child with my parents. We did a pilgrimage."

"I was hard-pressed to leave. It's such a spiritual place with ghosts and shrines everywhere."

"My family is Sufi, and we visited with some poets and went to many holy places. Varanasi isn't just special for Hindus, you know."

"I met a few Muslims at the university. They were very enlightened and artistic. The place felt a lot like home for me, except for the cold!"

Noor laughed. "You should come to England sometime if you want to feel the cold!"

"Well, Delhi was even colder than Varanasi. I never really felt comfortable there. It's a crazy place."

"Oh gosh, yes. Especially now."

"Indeed. You can't have a drink anywhere without someone breathing down your neck asking you which side you're on!"

She grimaced. "I know what you mean. At least this group here is more laid back."

"Yes, I like it here a lot. I was just going to pass through on my way home to Mysore, but now I'm thinking I may stay for a while."

"You should stay. I can show you around."

CHAPTER 9

Umesh and Noor began to spend a lot of time together. They visited museums, saw movies, went on boat rides around the harbor, and drove around in her father's Bentley. They frequently ended up alone together late into the night. He would play the flute for her, and she told him stories of her time in England.

"Did I tell you I'm supposed to go to Pune to get married? My poor groom has been waiting for years for me. I finally told him I wasn't a virgin, but it didn't make a difference. He still wants to marry me. Of course, it's all about my father's money."

He laughed. "Well, I beat you on that one. I'm already married!"

She slapped his hand playfully. "Now you tell me. Where's your wife?"

"Back in Mysore, waiting for me to come home."

She got up from her chair and came towards him. She took his hands and placed them on her hips.

"It seems to me that we both have a window of opportunity here." She started to sway her hips gently, holding his hands firmly on her sides.

Umesh rose slowly from his seat. He took her hands and raised them to his lips, looking straight into her eyes. He then led her to his bedroom, where they practiced all the moves they had learned in their collective travels. She was particularly interested in what the courtesans in Varanasi were like and made him show her all the special things they did. She was a very receptive student.

Months passed, with Umesh and Noor practically living together in his flat. Some days they barely left the bed. The mutual obligations to their respective families gave a delicious urgency to their time together. They both knew their affair would have to end, and they were intent on pushing the envelope as far as they could.

She was the first who had to give in.

"I think I have to go back to Pune finally."

"Why now? What is the rush?"

"My groom's family is getting a bit anxious."

"I bet they're getting worried about your age," he smiled sarcastically.

She threw her napkin at him.

"I'm sure you're right. They definitely want grandchildren."

"Well, it's going to take you at least a couple of weeks to get organized, packed, and ready to go, right?"

"Oh yes, it might even take a month!" Noor smiled, running her leg up and down Umesh's underneath the table they were sitting at for breakfast.

They spent the next month going to parties, dinners, and seeing friends. Their lovemaking took on a distinctly different tone in those last weeks. It was as if they had both mentally moved on from their relationship, and there was less and less abandon. At least they had made the most of their time together.

Once she was gone, Umesh thought it was time for him to move on as well. He sent a message home to his wife and mother that he would be leaving soon and should be back in Mysore within a week or so.

He did a lot of walking around those last days in Mumbai. He thought a lot about Noor, his wife in Mysore, and what he would do once he returned. Even though he had been a childhood friend of the Maharajah's nephew, who was now the new Maharajah, they hardly knew each other anymore. And anyway, he had no interest in taking a position in government or administration. He thought about all that time he had wasted studying pharmacy and working on all those new rules. He laughed to himself, thinking about all the bazaar druggists who probably hadn't even heard of the Drugs Act, still selling all kinds of counterfeit, dangerous, and useless powders, potions, and tonics. He thought he should do a little experiment. He wandered down to the main high street and found the most upmarket druggist shop, one with glass windows, a fancy display, and a British name.

"Good afternoon sir," the Indian clerk behind the counter said. "What can I help you with?"

"Oh, I am from the Drugs Commission, and I'm here to speak with the dispensing pharmacist."

The clerk looked puzzled.

"Sir, I don't know what you mean. What is a dispensing pharmacist?" The clerk could barely repeat the foreign phrase back to Umesh.

"Hmm, do you have a boss? Is the owner of the shop here?"

"No sir, he is not here. He comes here at the end of the day to close up and collect the money."

"OK then, maybe I will come back later to meet him."

He shook his head as he left the shop and carried on toward the closest bazaar market. It was a ten-minute walk. Once he turned off from the main street, he walked through the different areas of the bazaar until he reached the apothecary section.

There were about a dozen stalls on the street. Each had someone sitting outside, guarding the displays of soap, small tin boxes filled with various powders, and large urns filled with seeds and dried leaves. He wandered around the stalls, looking at the different brands and names on the various offerings, before finally stopping outside one of them.

"Greetings my friend. Are you the owner of this stall?"

"No sir, he is actually inside the shop right now."

Umesh walked past the copper scale and pushed aside the curtains blocking the view from the street. The inside of the shop was very small and cramped, barely five-foot square. The owner was a wizened old man, sitting cross-legged and barefoot on the floor. Behind him were shelves from floor to ceiling, all packed tightly with various tins and jars, most without any label whatsoever.

"Greetings, Old Father. I am looking for something for my friend. He needs some help in the bedroom, you know what I mean?" he winked.

The old man flashed a toothless smile. "Yes, yes, sir, always for your friend! I will give you something. This is coming from China, and they say if you are not careful, your wife won't be able to walk for a week!"

Umesh laughed. "Do you know what it is made from?"

"Oh, it is a secret, but I swear to you, you will be amazed at the power."

He bought a little pouch of the powder and moved on to the next stall. By the end of the afternoon, he'd gathered quite a collection, including calomel for malaria, santonin for worms, quinine pills, a few bars of Pears soap, some perfumes, cough medicine, and liver pills. He also picked up some betel leaves folded up over cocaine, a few ounces of cannabis, and a small vial of arsenic.

He then returned to the first shop to see if the owner was there.

"Hello, sir. How can I help you?"

"I am from the Drugs Commission. I wanted to ask you a few questions."

He could see the sudden tension in the man's face.

"Yes sir. What is the Drugs Commission?"

"Well, you may have heard, the government in Delhi is going to put some regulations into the drugs trade."

"Are you sure? I never heard such a thing."

"Well, it may take some time. It is a very new Act. It was passed about a year ago, in 1940."

"No sir. I don't know anything about this. How can I help you?" The man looked very suspicious and threatening.

"I was wondering, how do you stock up your shop with your goods? Do you buy your inventory from other merchants?"

"We are very lucky here. I just go down to the port. There is a broker there who knows what is arriving on which ships. I tell him what I want. Every time I am there, he also tells me about many new items. Then, after a few days, they will deliver everything to my shop. Everything comes to Mumbai first, direct from America, from Germany. My customers like to buy western goods."

Umesh brought his little shopping bag back to his apartment. In the space of a few hours, he had amassed drugs of every description, potency, and, he was sure, a few fake ones. All for a few rupees total. He was astounded at how cheap the items were. But he'd made his point to himself. No one had even heard of the Drugs Act of 1940. And given the complete absence of qualified dispensers, he was hard-pressed to understand how anyone could get a license under the requirements of the Act. He shook his head as he wrapped his purchases individually. He would bring them home. Perhaps his wife and his mother would appreciate some of the items. He doubted that such things would be so readily available in Mysore.

"You know we can get all of these things here in Mysore, and what you can't find here, you can certainly find in Bangalore." His mother was amused at the gifts he had brought back for them. "I can show you where you can buy even more unusual potions. Many products also come from America for cosmetics, coloring hair, and preventing boils and blemishes. Your wife has been buying some of them in anticipation of your return. I am just warning you that she is very anxious to get pregnant. She has been waiting three years now for you."

Umesh's father had died in 1937, just before he'd left Mysore for Varanasi. His wife Lathika had moved into his mother's residence after the wedding, and the two women had lived together since then. He wondered how that had all gone.

His wife was very young. He tried to remember her age when they had married but wasn't quite sure. He guessed she was about fifteen now.

"You've done a nice job setting up our rooms here. I know it must have been hard for you, living here with Mother on your own." He was stroking her naked back as they lay in bed.

"I'm so glad you finally came home. Your mother is a kind lady, but this apartment was furnished by her. You see, it's hard to disagree with her as long as I'm living in her house."

"You are such a good girl." He winked at her. "And so beautiful. I'd forgotten how lovely you are!"

"Now you are making fun of me," she laughed as she rolled over and climbed on top of him.

They spent many afternoons in bed, working diligently on making a baby. She didn't care what he did afterward as long as this was successful. Umesh didn't argue.

PART III
SURESHA DIVERSIFIES

CHAPTER 10

With Geetha's help, Suresha managed to avoid being robbed, scammed, and bribed of the money he had received from the Maharajah. Over the next fifteen years, he expanded from one pushcart into three separate stalls in different parts of the city. Since he didn't have a specific trade, he pursued an innovative strategy of setting up shops where a variety of items were sold, giving his clients the convenience of one-stop shopping. It had proved a very lucrative formula, particularly in a rapidly growing city like Bangalore. Everyone called him "Roseroyce."

They still lived in their single room in the oldest part of the city. Much to Geetha's satisfaction, her mother-in-law had finally died, and Girisha had married and moved out, so it was much less crowded. She had sent her sons to school, as Bina had always wanted, but her youngest succumbed to cholera or some similar disease; she had no idea. Now it was just the three of them. Suresha had tried hard to make another baby after his son died but to no avail. He was a bit mystified, not understanding why his still young wife could not get pregnant, but he never brought it up.

They didn't trust anyone but family to run the shops. So Girisha took care of the one in the train station, and Geetha ran the one just along the market street close to their room. Suresha managed the furthest one, on the other side of the station, at the Russell Market. He still had to rise before dawn each day to travel the distance to the stall.

Geetha watched the money coming in with a combination of elation and trepidation. On the one hand, she wanted nice things. After they had opened the third stall, she had dared to buy herself a new sari, bangles, and an ankle bracelet. She was also fascinated by all the new cosmetic products she found in the market, such as hair dyes, pencils, powders, and lipsticks, all in different colors and packages. Since she now controlled the money, she always spent a few pennies to try something new. And she still practiced her birth control in whatever way was available. But their money was sitting there, piling up, and she felt pressure; pressure to keep it safe and pressure to do something with it.

She was convinced they should branch out from selling just drinks, cigarettes, and a few household items. She had always watched with envy the amounts of money changing hands whenever she visited the apothecary shops. Even the poorest managed to show up with money to buy medicine for their sick children or parents. The women and girls especially wanted to know about ointments that made their skin clear of pimples. Each time Geetha visited the shop, the old man had new items to sell. She wondered if she could convince her husband to spend some money to see if it was a business they could get into. She had pushed him hard to open up the second and third shops; he would never have pursued the diversification without her bullying.

"I have something I want to discuss with you," she said soon after Suresha had returned from the market.

"Oh Geetha, I am tired and hungry. Can't it wait?" He was expecting another lecture about money.

"No, the timing is important."

"Fine then, what is it?"

"I think we should start selling apothecary products, you know, things like medicines, cough syrups, pills that cure people and make them feel better."

"You are joking. What do we know of such things?"

"It's not hard. There are at least ten stalls in the drugs market bazaar. Each one of them is doing a huge business every day. I can show you. And the people running the shops are all old. They know nothing of medicines, and they lie to everyone."

"But we are already so busy, we can hardly take care of our business now. You are talking about doing something more complicated and serious."

"Yes, but if you can become known for selling medicines, people will prefer to come to your shop because you are in the right places. They can buy their potions without going to the special place in the market, where many are ashamed to go."

"No, Geetha, not now. I can't imagine adding this to our work."

"Sooner or later someone else will have this idea. We should be the first to do it. We can make enough money to send your son to university and maybe find a better place to live."

She didn't care much about her son going to college but knew Suresha did. She was keen to leave the slum and get a couple of rooms in a nice apartment building. One that had an outhouse, a front door, and proper stairs.

But she dropped the subject for now. Patience, she told herself. Her husband was a man who liked his routine, and his feathers got ruffled easily, like if dinner was a few minutes late, if she placed his slippers near the bottom of the bed instead of the top, or if she put out a clean shirt for him in the morning without warning him the night before.

Geetha thought it would be good for him to go to the drugs bazaar to see for himself the goings-on. She wouldn't go with him, though. The shopkeepers would recognize her for sure. She waited a few days before bringing it up again.

"You know, the drugs bazaar is on the way to the Russell Market. Tomorrow you should stop there on your way home and see for yourself. You will be amazed how busy they are."

"Geetha, do you understand how tired I am when I am on the way home? I'm not going there because this is not a good idea, and I won't give in to your schemes."

It took him five days before he decided to do her bidding. He had been thinking a lot about her assertions that this new venture would bring in more money, maybe enough to send his son to college. He also remembered the last time he had visited Bina's apartment, how nice and comfortable the rooms were, how bright, no smell from the latrines, and how the class of people around her was different. It couldn't hurt just to go and have a look.

CHAPTER 11

Suresha locked up his stall at the end of the day and set out to find the drugs bazaar. He splurged on a rickshaw for the journey, which he would normally travel on foot. When he stepped off the cart, he looked around, not exactly sure which way to go. The bazaar in the old town was huge, and he had to find his way through the different sections to get to the right place. He stopped a young boy on the street.

"Hey, you, do you know where the drugs bazaar is?"

"Yes, sir, yes, I know exactly where it is. Can I show you the way?"

He rolled his eyes. There was no way to ask for help anywhere in Bangalore without someone holding their hand out for money. Even if they didn't know what you were looking for.

"Are you sure you know it? I don't believe you."

"But sir, I go there all the time. My mother and her neighbors are always sending me there. My uncles give me money to buy them special things that they don't want to ask for themselves. I know this place very well."

"What kind of things?"

"I'm not sure. When they ask me to go, they always say to ask for the special medicine for men."

"What does that mean?"

"Don't you know? It is for help when you are in bed with your wife. The shopkeepers always laugh at me when I ask for this medicine."

Suresha wasn't entirely sure what the child meant. He was intrigued to hear he could take something that would give him a boost when making love to Geetha. Maybe he should try it.

They went through the back alleys until they reached the entrance of the drugs bazaar. He didn't want the boy shadowing him here, so he gave him a rupee to get rid of him, but it still took several minutes before the youngster stopped following him.

He looked around. There were about a dozen stalls, most with beaded curtains covering the entrance in a feeble attempt at privacy. The street was busy with people.

Suresha walked up to the first stall and pushed the curtain aside.

"Good afternoon, my dear friend. What can I help you with? I must say, you are looking a bit yellow, and your eyes are cloudy. Let me show you this powder. You mix it with some water and drink it. In a few days your skin will be shiny and your eyes clear. Here come, only three rupees for one week's supply."

There was a makeshift counter inside the shop. The shopkeeper was a young, chubby man missing a few front teeth.

"And what happens after one week?"

"Well, of course, you have to come back. I will give you a discount when you become my customer." The man smiled.

"Where did you get this medicine?"

"Oh, I have been selling this one for many years now. I can vouch for it with many other customers. I get it from the wholesale market near the train station. But I also have this brand-new elixir. If you take it, you will be amazed at how it clears the mind. You will look and feel like a young man again."

Suresha looked at him suspiciously. No one had ever accused him of looking old.

"And how much for the clear mind elixir?"

"That one is more expensive. It is a new one, from Germany. Five rupees."

He told the man he would think about it.

"Well, you never know; I may run out of it next week. You should really at least try it."

Suresha didn't answer and walked out of the stall. Three women were waiting outside to go in. He hadn't noticed the shopkeeper had pushed a small red flag through a slot in the front of the stall when he had entered, indicating that he was with a customer. He saw it disappear into the shop as he left.

Very clever, he thought to himself.

As he moved down the street, he noticed many of the stalls had six or seven people waiting to go in, all eyes watching the little red flags. He never had people waiting in line to come into his stalls. By now he was very intrigued.

A few shops down, he stopped. Only three people were in line here: one old woman and two young boys. He stood behind them, patiently waiting his turn.

He examined the outside of the shop. A dirty, hand-scrawled sign was in front, but he could not read it. Hanging from the outside were bundles of roots, little plastic bags full of a green powder, and several sticks tied from one end in a long chain. A young woman in a bright red sari came out of the shop. She had a ring in her nose, and her hair was braided with flowers tied all along the plait.

Suresha stopped her.

"Greetings, sister. I am wondering, can you tell me if this shopkeeper is an honest man?"

She looked at him suspiciously.

"What do you mean?"

"Well, I need some medicine for my mother. She is very old and has a lot of pain in her knees. She can't walk anymore." He remembered the last days of his mother, laying on her blankets, riddled with pain, her eyes glassy, her breath coming out in rasping waves.

"Why don't you ask the medicine man inside to help you? I don't know about such things."

"Well, I want to make sure I don't get cheated."

The woman shrugged her shoulders and walked on. It was clear she wanted to get away as quickly as possible.

The old woman went in next. He thought she might prove to be more talkative. He accosted her as she walked by him on her way out.

"Grandmother, what did you buy today?" he asked, smiling.

She flashed a toothless smile back.

"Do you need a girl? I have a lot of girls in my room, you can come and see. I have many young ones who will make you very happy."

"No, no, I am not looking for that. I am just curious since you were in the shop a long time. What did you buy?"

"That is not your concern. I have to take care of my girls. I am going now."

Finally, he got his turn. This shop was a bit more spacious than the last. There were two counters, and the shopkeeper came to meet him from a back room.

"Hello, sir, what do you look for today?"

Suresha repeated the story about his mother.

"Well, you know, if she is in a lot of pain, the best thing is to give her this powder, which is very strong but will help her to sleep."

"What is it?"

"It is made from opium. Many of my customers take it for their aches and pains."

"Opium?" Suresha was a newcomer to this world.

"Yes, do you know it? It is a drug that makes you feel good. All your troubles disappear. If your wife is nagging you too much or if you are worried about something, it helps you to forget."

"Is it very expensive?"

"No, only two rupees for a bag." The bag was very small.

"I'm not sure if it will help."

"Trust me, sir, she will thank you for this. This is a drug I sell to many of my customers. They are always coming back for more, some of them every day."

"Can you buy this in the other stalls?"

"No, no, of course not. I am the only one selling this. You must buy from me only." The man leaned back, holding his hands up in the air.

"Where do you get this opium?"

"Listen, do you want to buy it or not? I don't have time to waste with you. I have many customers waiting."

Suresha left the stall empty-handed.

As he walked down the road, he saw the young woman in the red sari walking a few meters in front of him. He ran up to her and gently pulled at her elbow.

"Hi, miss, can you tell me where I can buy some opium?"

The woman looked at him, recognizing him from her previous stop.

"Why are you following me? I told you to leave me alone."

"But sister, my mother is very ill, and she has a lot of pain. I need to buy some opium for her. I don't know where to get it."

"Stupid man, you can buy it in any of these shops on this road. Now stop bothering me."

CHAPTER 12

Suresha was starting to see what Geetha meant. The shops were selling things he had never heard of, or even seen before. There was a whole array of weird powders, pills, and liquids that seemed to cater to any type of ailment, real or imagined. The shopkeepers were good at convincing their customers of the importance of what they were selling, and the clients seemed very willing to buy whatever was being offered to them. And they kept coming back. He was impressed.

But it was hard to know where to get the inventory these people were selling. And they were unwilling to share any secrets, especially ones that might increase the competition. If he was going to get in on this venture, there was a lot of work to be done. Suresha was not convinced they had the time or the courage to get involved in this. But it was tempting. Maybe he could get his son to run one of the shops for a few weeks while he spent some time figuring out this business. But he had tried to get his son to help before and wasn't optimistic. Perhaps Geetha could make him do it, even if just for a few days until he could figure out if this was going to work.

"I went to see the crazy drugs bazaar today on the way home. You are right; it is quite a place. Lots of customers buying things I don't understand. One shopkeeper tried to sell me something called opium, which takes all the pain away. Have you heard of this?"

"Opium is very good, but it is easy to become addicted. One needs to be careful. But many other medicines can help with pain, coughs, colds, toothache, and headaches."

"Geetha, how do you know about all this?"

"Oh, my mother knew a lot about it. She told me a few things."

"I tried to find out where I could buy the medicines, but no one would tell me. Somewhere at the train station. I don't know where to get them."

"You can just go and buy from these stalls, bring them to your shop and sell them. I am telling you, if one doesn't have to travel to the drugs market but can buy from your stall, you will see, you can charge enough to make a profit."

Suresha was continually surprised by his wife's resourcefulness.

"Once you start selling the items, I am sure you will be able to make contact with the bigger sellers."

"Maybe I can go to the station and ask a few questions. I am sure it's all coming here by train."

"Yes, that is a good idea. I will tell our son to manage the shop for one day while I go to the drugs bazaar and buy some things for you. Then you can put them in the shops and see what happens. You just have to let your customers know that you have these items."

"Most people coming to our shops buy small things to eat or drink. I don't think they will be interested in medicine."

"Just wait and see." Geetha knew better. She was sure that once word got around that you could buy medicine from the local stall, customers would show up.

After much coaxing, threatening, and cajoling, she got her son to spend a day in the shop while she went to the bazaar. She carefully measured out how much money she thought she would need, and set off to get some merchandise. She had thought a great deal about what she would buy, trying to relate the types of customers coming to their stalls to the sorts of medicines she would get.

She bought one sleeve of pills for diarrhea, quinine pills for malaria, a few small vials of cough medicine, and a good-sized bag of opium powder. She also found liver pills, which were supposed to improve the skin color, and she bought a small bottle of special medicine that would get rid of warts. She planned to break up the opium powder into small bundles, and they would, of course, sell each pill individually.

Geetha showed Suresha her stash that evening.

"I will bring these to my shop here tomorrow. Let's see what happens over the coming days, and we can decide what to do next." Geetha was quickly taking charge of this new venture.

Her first customer was a young girl who came every morning to buy three cigarettes for her husband. He would have given her money the night before, since he was paid at the end of each day for his work on a building site. She always arrived early so he could have them for the rest of the day. Geetha had noticed the warts on her knuckles. She was ready when she arrived.

"Look, I have found this medicine for your ugly warts. I even tried it myself, and they disappeared after a few days. If you want, I can put some on your fingers. Only one rupee. Then I can put some more on tomorrow when you come."

The girl hid her hands shyly but was very curious.

"Do you think this will make them go away?"

"Yes, just try it for a few days. I am sure it will work."

Geetha pulled the three cigarettes from the pack and brought the tincture out from behind her counter.

"Here, hold your hands out. I will put one drop on each one."

The girl held her hand out while Geetha smeared a single drop over all the warts.

"There. Tomorrow we can decide if we put some more on."

After paying, the girl walked out of the stall with her hands outstretched, expecting the drops would have instantaneously done their magic.

Geetha had bought the bottle of wart medicine for four rupees. She should be able to get at least twenty or more doses out of it. At one rupee each, that was a tidy sum.

The next day, when the girl arrived, Geetha asked her to show her her hands.

"Oh yes, I see an improvement. This wart on your ring finger is definitely drying out."

The girl examined her hands for probably the hundredth time since getting the drops the day before.

"I'm not sure, but I think you are right. I see a little bit of different color on the sides."

"Well, of course, we need to apply it again. It may take a few days to cure you completely."

The drops were added to the daily routine of the cigarette purchase. There was no change whatsoever in the girl's warts, but she was easily persuaded by a few compliments. She had told several of her neighbors and relatives that Geetha was selling medicine. By the end of the week, she had run out of her supply.

She reported all this to Suresha daily. He was by now keen to try this out in his stall, which was far busier than Geetha's. He had already made a few mental notes about some of his regulars, one with a limp, another with an open sore on his arm that never healed, and a third whose eyes were constantly weeping and oozing.

"You need to go back to the bazaar and get me a few more things to sell. Tomorrow, I will stop at the train station and ask around to see if there is some way to find the items. This has to be the way the medicines are coming to Bangalore."

Geetha had brought in a lot of money from the trial run. Suresha felt confident enough to close his stall early the following day and headed over to the station. First, he stopped in to see his brother at the stall.

"Hey, Girisha, how is business today?"

"Ah, Suresha, good of you to come. I am doing OK. Is there a problem? I have given you all the money from last week already."

"No, no problem. I am here to check something out. I'm going to see my broker who sells me all the stock for our stalls, to ask him a few questions."

"Well, be careful. That man is a thief. He comes to the stall at least once a week, asking me if I need more supplies. I tell him no, but he is always nosing around, telling me I'm running out of this or that. Then he asks me how much I am selling things for, and I tell him if you want to know then just buy it!"

Suresha laughed.

"You are doing a good job, Girisha. I know this is a very busy place, and you have the most customers of all."

"Well, I don't mind the work. I have so many regular customers now. They come here every day because they know I give them a special price."

"How are your boys?"

"They are good, getting big, and they look very healthy."

"Good, good. Well, I am off to find Ramu." He steadied himself, as dealing with this man was always fraught with dishonesty and deception.

CHAPTER 13

Ramu was a big, fat man. The bottom three buttons of his shirt would not close over his belly, and he walked with a limp. He had a bushy mustache and small, bloodshot eyes. Suresha had been afraid of him ten years ago when they first met, but over the years they had forged a mutually beneficial, albeit cautious, relationship.

"Ah, Roseroyce, what are you doing here today? I thought you had enough supply for the coming weeks."

"Hi, Ramu. Yes, I do, I do. I am here to talk business with you."

"No more discounts for you, Mr. Roseroyce. You are already getting the best price from me. And I am always showing you the new things that are coming, you know this."

"Yes, yes. I know all this. But I am curious. Do you know something about the items that are sold in the drugs bazaar?"

"Why, did someone cheat you? You must be very careful in that place. They are all deceivers and cheats."

"Why do you say that?"

"They are buying anything they get their hands on. They come here and buy whatever comes off the train: pills, packets, powders and liquids, everything. No one can read. No one knows what is what. The wholesalers are basically running an auction, standing by the side of the train, and people are just bidding. You know, these things are sometimes even made of chalk and sugar. No one can tell."

"But those guys in the drugs market are doing a very good business. If they are selling sugar, don't people realize it?"

"Of course not. Everyone wants a miracle drug, and everyone wants these fancy names from Germany and England. If you tell some stupid poor person his medicine is coming from Japan, he will pay twice as much. Especially if you tell him it will make him perform better in bed. But the women are worse than the men."

"What do you mean?"

"They are always hoping to make themselves more beautiful, to smell good, to paint their faces. I know because my wife is spending a lot of money on such things."

"Ramu, what if I wanted to get some of these products? Can you sell them to me or do I have to go to someone else?" Suresha carefully asked.

"What? Why do you want to buy these? Your stalls are not in the drugs bazaar."

"I don't have to be in the drugs bazaar to sell the items. And I'm told many are embarrassed to go there."

"This may be true, but you need a good friend to guide you through this. It is a tough business."

Suresha knew what was coming next.

"I can help you, but I need a good commission if I do this for you. Fifty percent of what you buy."

"Come on, I can walk down this platform and find ten like you who will show me where to get what I want. Surely you don't think I am new to this business?" He could tell Ramu was not well known to the drugs brokers and was hedging his bets.

Ramu studied his adversary, carefully thinking about what to say next.

"Why don't we go see what is going on; then we can discuss this once you have found what you want."

"That is a good idea."

They walked through the station, out the back, and headed for a dilapidated warehouse just a few steps behind the tracks.

"They bring the goods from Mumbai mostly. Then they unload them from the train and bring them here to this place. I have never been inside, but I know this is where they sell the medicines that are coming from Europe and America, and even Japan."

They went in. It was late in the day, and it was pretty quiet. Suresha saw several large plastic tubs filled with various colored pills, just piled loose, as if they were flowers from the flower market. There were boxes packed with square cakes of soap, little dropper bottles filled with a brown liquid, and a few large blue plastic containers with taps set at the bottom.

"Greetings, sirs, I am pleased to help you. I have not seen you before as one of my regulars."

"No, we are just curious to see what you have to offer."

"Well, come let me show you what I have. All these items came from Mumbai yesterday. We get a shipment almost twice a month. Each time I have to tell them to bring more. Nowadays we always need more, as everyone is running out sooner and sooner."

The salesman led the way to the back of the warehouse.

"What are you looking for? I have all the ordinary stuff: quinine, calomel, medicines for people who have trouble breathing, pills for kidney pain, pills for liver pain, and cod liver oil. I also have some new items that are now becoming very popular. Here is a medicine to put on warts. This one is to help with a cough, and there is also a new tablet for getting rid of worms. You can now just take a tablet instead of looking everywhere for the powder. It is very easy to swallow."

He held one up. It was a large, pink-colored, chalky tablet. It didn't look easy to swallow to Suresha.

"I will give you a good discount if you buy a big amount. How much do you want?"

Suresha didn't want to take on too much product, at least not until they had proven that the demand was there. And he didn't have that much space in his stalls. Ramu was standing close behind him, making sure he could hear the conversation.

"Look, I don't want to buy a big quantity, but I want to buy many different items. If they sell well, then I will come back for more."

"Where is your stall my friend, can I ask? Are you in the drugs bazaar?"

"No, I am not located there." He didn't want to disclose anything more.

"Well, then, as long as you are not talking to those guys in the bazaar, I can make you a price for a sample of almost everything. You should also take some soaps." He picked up a round, orange-colored bar. "You can even cut these in half and they will sell. These are British soaps, very popular. I will make a price for you."

Geetha had spent about ten rupees in the drugs bazaar. Suresha had come with a hundred and planned to spend fifty or sixty. This dealer was the only place to get a decent volume. He had to convince him he would be back for more.

They wandered through the rows of supplies, and Suresha bought a dozen of most of the pills. These were wrapped into separate bundles. He also wanted some of the medicine for coughs, some of the one for warts, and a dozen bars of soap.

"Do you have any opium?" he asked the dealer.

"Oh, I have all kinds of this. I have a powder you can mix with water. I also have a potion that is good for babies. It tastes good, and another one is for women when they are bleeding."

Suresha turned red from embarrassment.

"I'll take some of each."

The dealer put all the items in a bag. He got a couple of small glass dropper bottles and filled them with the medicine from the vats.

"Now you remember the color of the pills for the different problems, right? And the opium tincture for the babies has a drawing of a baby on it. This is how you can tell."

"Fine, fine, yes, I remember. I'll give you twenty rupees."

"No, no. This is a small amount. I am not giving you a wholesale price for this. This is sixty."

"Listen, I am telling you I will be back in a week for more supply. If you are going to charge me a normal price, I will just go buy it from the drugs bazaar. You have to make this worth my while."

"OK, fifty-five."

"No, I am willing to pay you thirty but no more."

It was the end of the day. Suresha was a new customer, and the dealer was probably wondering if he would be back.

"Make it forty then and you can take them."

"OK, that is good, I agree."

As they walked out of the warehouse, Suresha pulled a couple of rupees out of his pocket and gave them to Ramu.

"Look, I need much more than this for the help I gave you. I think you have to pay me at least twice that amount."

"That is all I am giving you, so either you can be happy or you can be sad. But either way, there is no more commission for you." Suresha smiled. He turned and started the journey home before the broker could say anything more.

Geetha and Suresha studied their acquisitions. Suresha wanted to bring some to Girisha the very next day. He was sure the stall would sell out quickly once word got out that medicine was available there. Geetha portioned out the pills. She had saved the empty wart medicine dropper and poured some of the cough liquid into it.

"People can just take a swallow from the bottle. You can easily charge two or three rupees, depending on the size of the person's mouth."

"That's a good idea. We can save all the empty bottles and use them to distribute the supply to the stalls."

CHAPTER 14

A few weeks later, Geetha brought a new bottle of wart medicine and a few face powders and lipsticks to her stall. She was waiting for her customer to arrive in the morning.

"Good morning, Sunita. How are you today?"

She was not surprised at the black eye and swollen lip. At least once a month, this was the way the girl arrived at her shop.

"Look, I have something for you. This is a powder. If you put a small amount on your face around your eye, it will cover the bruise until it heals. Really. Do you want me to show you?"

The girl looked at Geetha and raised her eyebrows.

"Yes, do you think it will look better?"

"Well, I can show you in this mirror how it looks now." She took a small mirror from the back of the counter and held it up to the girl. She gazed at herself, laughing a bit when she saw the black skin underneath her eye, and the reddish patch where his hand had landed on the side of her face.

"Here, try this." Geetha took a small box of pressed powder and dabbed a bit on the girl's face.

"There, that looks so much better!"

The girl peered at herself in the mirror, examining the smeared substance that made her bruise look gray instead of black.

"Listen, don't hold the mirror so close. That is not how others will look at you. Here, hold it back a bit. You see, it does look much less noticeable." She grabbed the mirror from the girl and held it back from her face.

"But Geetha, it must be very expensive. I can't afford such a thing. My husband only gives me money each day for the meals and his cigarettes."

"Oh, it's not very expensive. And it will last you a long time if you only use it when needed. I can let you pay for it over a few weeks if you want it. Here, let's put the medicine on your fingers now."

She dabbed some of the new wart medicine on the girl's hands and sent her on her way.

Sunita came back the next morning for her daily purchases. As soon as she got to the stall, she showed Geetha her fingers. The warts were blistered and oozing. Nothing like this had happened before when she had first taken the medicine.

"Geetha, look, look at my fingers. They are burning!" She was scared.

"Oh, don't worry, Sunita, it looks to me like the medicine is starting to work now. You will see, in a few days finally the warts will be gone."

Geetha put some more drops on the girl's fingers and sent her on her way. She wondered what was different about the medicine since the previous bottle hadn't done a thing to the warts. After a whole week of applying the new liquid, the warts started to crumble and turn white. The girl's fingers didn't look much better than when they had started the treatment; the warts had been replaced by white, dried-up, sunken craters on her knuckles. But Geetha easily convinced the girl that the medicine had done its job.

"Now that your warts are cured, you can spend this money on something else, something nice for yourself. Look at this: it is a soap. Have you ever used soap before? Here, see how nice it smells!"

Geetha and Suresha strategized every night on price and quantity. Geetha's stall was selling items at lower prices because of its location in the slums. The high street near their room was much less busy now than ten years ago. Girisha's stall at the train station was charging more for everything, and he was always selling out. The shop at the Russell Market was the most expensive. It was where all the British and Europeans came shopping, and they always had more money in their pockets. A white face was synonymous with being rich.

Suresha was stocking more and more medicines and potions and allocating less and less space to the sundry items he used to sell. Within a year, he'd switched over entirely to selling pills and drugs, and also cosmetics, and all kinds of therapeutic mysteries. The amount of product coming in was astounding. Each week, new items were available, and he was having a difficult time keeping everything straight. He had started to bring his son with him to help write out and label all the different things he was buying. He had to bribe him to help by giving him money and promising to send him to university. But they argued all the time.

Suresha arrived home to find his son getting ready to go out.

"Where are you going? I was going to talk to you about helping Girisha in the shop. Of the three, it is the busiest by far."

"Father, I have to go to a rally. We are marching to protest the British."

"Again? How many times do you have to do this before you learn you are wasting your time?" He didn't understand his son's obsession with politics.

"When I was your age, I was already working in the flower market. What do you do all day now? We are paying for you to go to school. You should know I expect some work in return."

"Can we talk about this later? I have to go now." His son was used to his father's rants, and he had learned the best response was just to walk away.

"He'd better not get into any trouble," Suresha muttered to Geetha. "Last week I heard they put some people in jail for throwing stones at the post office."

"Your son wouldn't do such a thing. Anyway, I told him to be careful. Did he tell you he wants to go to college? He wants to study to be a teacher."

"He's crazy. He won't even be accepted. And anyway, who is going to pay for this?"

"He knows there is money."

"How does he know that? He wouldn't know if he didn't see you buying clothes and trinkets."

"I don't buy such things. But your son is not blind."

Suresha pursed his lips and shook his head. "He needs to help us with the shops. He can't just go running off with his angry friends."

"I don't think your son will be a shopkeeper. This is what happens when they learn to read and write. They always want more. This is the curse we got by sending him to school like your sister wanted."

He didn't answer. He knew sending his son to school had been the right thing to do. But Geetha was right; the more he was educated, the more he looked down on his family's way of life.

CHAPTER 15

By the time the war was over, Suresha's three shops were doing a huge business selling drugs. Geetha kept nagging him about moving to a better place, and complaining that she didn't want to work in the shop anymore. He needed someone to man her stall while she went around looking for a new home, but his son was in university and had absolutely no interest in helping out. Geetha told him to talk to Girisha, who had two sons. The eldest, Kumara, was almost fifteen, but Suresha wasn't so confident that his nephew could handle it. His left arm was shriveled from birth, his three fingers bent into a claw, and Suresha was sure that he wasn't normal in the head.

"But my shop is not as busy as the other two. You know that. It was the first stall we opened, and the business is much less today. I am sure Kumara can handle it. And I can keep an eye on him and make sure he does the job the way we want."

"But do you think he has enough brains to do the job?"

"What do you mean? You were already working when you were this age, and Girisha also. Kumara is a good boy. He has no delusions about going to university, and he never got involved in all that rock-throwing during the Quit India campaign, like your son. And his brain is perfectly adequate for the work."

Suresha still had his doubts, but he eventually gave in. He would at least try it. If it didn't work, they would figure out something else.

As soon as her nephew was settled into the stall, Geetha started to look for a new place to live. She knew she couldn't afford to live close to Bina, and anyway, she wasn't sure she would want to see her every day. Her objective was to get out of the slum area and find a couple of rooms in one of the new concrete buildings being built all over Bangalore. One had to climb stairs, but it seemed to her that being high up was very desirable. There was some privacy, and the rooms were quite a bit bigger than theirs. The downside was that she would have to carry water up to her rooms every day. As long as her son was living with them, he could do this chore for her. And she was keen to get one of those new iron stoves she'd seen in the market.

She finally settled on a building not far from Cubbon Park. They took a two-room apartment on the third floor of a brand-new construction. She bought a new mattress and sheets for their bed. Suresha complained bitterly for days after they moved; everything was in a different place than he was used to, and his commuting routine was completely disrupted. But Geetha was very satisfied.

Slowly, the forces of government regulation were gathering in the background. Anger over the flood of adulterated and fake medicines was mounting in the years leading up to independence, and the bureaucracy in Delhi finally managed to issue an unwieldy document in the 1940 Drugs Act, followed by another set of statutes in 1945. The ambitious policies were designed to protect the public, but adoption and enforcement would be a long and arduous journey. The drug trade had infiltrated into every corner of India. Any efforts at control would be hindered by the challenges of communication across an enormous country and a shortage of qualified pharmacists and physicians.

It took a long time for all this to catch up with Suresha and his business. It wasn't until 1951 that he started to hear rumors and whispers about new rules that would soon be enforced around buying and selling drugs and medicines in his shops. The first sign was when the trader at the train station asked him for his license when he arrived to pick up his inventory for the month.

"What license? What are you talking about?"

"No, no, it's true. You need a license to buy this now."

Suresha had to deal with his prices and bribes going up each year, and he just assumed this was a new twist on the old story.

"I'll give you half a percent more on what I buy. Nothing more."

"That will just cover my risk if you don't have a license. I have to see your license next time."

"What license, you fool? What is this?"

"This is the new rule. My boss told me everyone who comes to buy must show a license."

"You are making this up. I never heard of this. Maybe you need a license to sell also?"

The man looked embarrassed. "Oh, I don't know about that."

"Well, you'd better ask. If I have to show you a license then you must need one too!" Suresha was fuming.

"Do you believe this nonsense? The man has no shame, asking me for a license to justify his bribe!" he later shouted at Geetha as soon as he walked into the apartment.

"Calm down. I don't understand what you're talking about."

"He wanted to see my license. Can you believe this? A license?"

"Did you ask him where you can get such a thing? He must know something to bring this up now?"

"No, no, no, he is just saying this to get more money. There is no license. He thinks we are ignorant and that we will just believe him and pay."

"Yes, but it is a strange thing for him to say suddenly. Maybe I will go to the drugs bazaar tomorrow and snoop around."

"You do whatever you want. I am telling you, it's just another bribe."

The following day, Geetha made the journey to the drugs bazaar to see her usual shopkeeper.

"Ah madam, you are back. I have kept for you the seeds you are always buying. Here, here it is for you all packaged up."

"Old man, you can open it. I want to see what you have put inside."

"Why? After all this time you've been my customer, you don't trust me?"

"You can be sure I don't trust you!" She smiled at the man, hoping to put him at ease. "Listen, I have to ask you something. Has anyone asked you for your license?"

"Ah, this is my new headache. They are telling all the drug traders that we will need to have a license within two years. One has to make an application, sign the form, and, of course, pay money. Most of the traders in this market won't bother, but we will have to pay something more to the wholesaler. But this is normal. With the independence, there will now be all kinds of new rules. But no one knows when they will start. It may take years for the papers to come back from the government."

Geetha took her bundle and moved down the row of shops to check on the man's story.

When Suresha returned home that evening, she reported on her findings.

"Well, I heard a lot of different stories. One said yes, they will need a license, but they are giving them two years to get it. Another said the rules will never reach Bangalore, and he just has to pay the wholesaler more money. The last I heard, this is just the beginning. He said one day they will make us get a doctor with western medicine to agree that we are selling the drugs with his permission."

"Ah, it's just a rumor. We are doing such a big business that everyone suddenly wants part of the action. Anyway, there are so few doctors in Bangalore. How do they think every single person who is selling drugs is going to do this?"

"You are right, but we need to find a way to get the true information, so that we are prepared."

PART IV
VIJAY

CHAPTER 16

Suresha was very pleased with Kumara's progress. The boy was very smart with his figures and had made many changes to the displays outside the shop to entice more customers. He had also painted some big signs with red crosses on them, which they had hung outside the stalls. "This is a universal symbol of apothecary and medical products," he had said. "It will announce to all the passers-by that we are selling the medicines."

Their stall in the old city was getting less and less traffic, while the one at the train station was doing a huge business, and Girisha was a bit overwhelmed. In fact, they could keep the stall open all night, and there would be a steady stream of customers. Kumara felt the slower pace of Geetha's original stall was much better suited for his father. After all, both his father and uncle were getting old. He had lately noticed that his uncle was walking with a limp and occasionally would close the shop at the Russell Market early and pay for a rickshaw to take him home. It made him think about the time that would come when both brothers would no longer be able to work.

He decided to visit his uncle to talk about this.

"Uncle, I think I can run all three shops for you from now on."

"Are you crazy? How do you think you can do that?"

"I will have my brother manage the shop for you at the Russell Market. I will keep working in the station, but I will also do all the shopping for you for the inventory. My father can take care of the shop in the old city. It is an easier job for him."

"But how can you run the busiest shop and at the same time manage all the inventory? It is a huge business for us now, and Geetha is helping me keep track of all the comings and goings with the figures, but it is a lot of work. And Vijay is just a boy!"

"Yes, but he is a very good boy, and he is anxious to work in the business. You can help me at the train station while I handle the purchases. That is a good solution for now. And Auntie can teach me the accounts and the ledgers."

Suresha calmed down a bit, realizing that his nephew was not suggesting that he retire abruptly from the business but rather tweak the responsibilities to afford him some time off. He smiled.

"You are very clever. You remind me of Geetha with all her ideas. We can try this for a while and see how things go."

Geetha listened to the exchange. Her husband had been struggling with fatigue for the last several months. His leg was becoming very lame, and he huffed and puffed coming up the stairs to their apartment. She had been thinking about how to convince him to reduce his workload. It was good Kumara had beaten her to it. Better to come from him than her.

"That boy is smart," he told her after Kumara had left. "His lame arm does him no disadvantage."

"We need to keep a close eye on him, though. He must not think the shops belong to him."

He looked sharply at her.

"Do you think we can trust him? Are you worried?"

"Well, let's just say we should be cautiously optimistic."

Suresha studied her face before answering, wondering if they were making the right decision.

"You are right, Geetha, always right."

Kumara's brother Vijay was five years younger than him and was already helping in the stores, running errands and messages between the three locations. If he installed Vijay in the store at Russell Market, they would eventually need a runner, but he could get by for a while until his uncle decided to retire completely from working the shop. He would start training him straight away.

Vijay was very excited when he learned of the plan. He was very keen to be taken seriously, and this promotion from being the errand boy was very welcome.

"You should plan to relieve Uncle in the early afternoons so he can go home and rest. That will allow you to run the errands in the morning. But you will have to be very careful to be on time. Uncle will be judging us both on this experiment, so you must be very conscious of the time and not get carried away by silly things on the way."

"You know I am going to make you proud of me. How will you manage the purchases if you are going to work in the train station?"

"Well, right now, Uncle is buying supplies once a month. I think we will, from now on, stock up every two or three weeks. If I am at the station, once you relieve Uncle from the Russell Market, he can come take over from me while I get the inventory. Doing it this way will take less time."

"And I can then help you to transfer the stock to the three shops."

"Yes, you will be quite busy. You are sure I will have your attention on this job?"

"Yes, you can count on me!" He puffed up his skinny twelve-year-old chest.

Kumara tousled his hair, smiling. "We are going to make a good team."

In the following weeks, the brothers got down to business. Kumara generally got to the train station by five in the morning. His goal was eventually to keep that shop open all the time. It was always busy. Both departing and arriving passengers were likely to visit his shop for headache medicine, asthma pills, soaps, tonics, and sundry other items to help them sleep, stay awake, for diarrhea, constipation, nausea, and whatever else travelers suffered.

Vijay would get to the station shop around nine in the morning, having already visited the Russell Market shop. He would carry any messages and requests for transfers of items. He would then run to the old city shop to check in with his father before returning to the Russell Market to relieve Suresha by early afternoon. He traveled a great distance each day by foot, which was fine for the energetic twelve-year-old. He saw and heard a lot on his journeys, bringing news of movies, shops, protests, and rallies to the family. He was like a human newspaper.

The last time Vijay was at the City Market, Geetha was there visiting with his father.

"So how is this business going? You and Kumara are doing a good job!"

"Thank you, Auntie. Things are going well."

"Are you walking and running between the three shops every single day?"

"For now yes, Auntie. Kumara says that soon maybe I won't have to go to each shop every day."

"It's true," Girisha said. "This shop is doing less and less business during the daytime."

"Why don't you get a bicycle?" Geetha asked.

"Oh, that would be very expensive, huh?"

"Anyway, he doesn't know how to ride one!" Girisha laughed.

"But surely he can learn. If he did this, he could even move some of the product around."

Geetha pursed her lips and shook her head. She swore under her breath that if she didn't keep track of these men, nothing would improve.

"Girisha, when you see Kumara later tonight, tell him I said he should get a bicycle for Vijay. It's OK to spend the money."

Vijay was thrilled when he left the shop. There were many cyclists on the roads in Bangalore these days, and he never imagined that he would join their ranks. He studied all the bicycles that passed him on the journey to the Russell Market. He couldn't wait.

The brothers went to the bazaar to buy a bicycle. They visited six stalls to compare prices. The most expensive ones came from America and Japan, but eventually, they settled on a used one made in Calcutta. Vijay stepped on the pedal, and as he lifted his other leg over the seat as he had watched others do over the last few days, he fell to the ground with the bicycle on top of him.

Kumara laughed.

"Are you hurt? Are you OK?"

Vijay got straight up, a little embarrassed and dazed.

"I'm OK, I'm OK."

This time, he held onto the bike and kept his right leg on the ground as he swung his left leg over the seat. He was trying to figure out what to do next when the trader who sold it to them was at his side on another bike.

"Here, watch me." He straddled the bike and slowly pushed the pedal with his left leg. As he started moving, he lifted his right leg off the ground onto the right pedal.

Vijay imitated the motions but only got a short distance before he wobbled and fell back onto the road. It only took a couple more runs before he figured out his balance, and he was able to ride in front of Kumara on the way back to their room, stopping frequently to let his brother catch up to him and take a breath.

With his new bicycle, Vijay could make his rounds in less than a third of the time it used to take him to walk. He would weave in and out of the crowds, dodging cows and chickens on the road. He even started racing tuk-tuks, chasing and often passing them on the road. Within a few months, Suresha was able to leave the shop around four in the afternoon. He would go home, and after a nice hot meal, he would take a nap. It had taken him some time to learn the art of doing nothing, but with his asthma and general physical malaise, he was quite relieved with the semi-retirement his two nephews had afforded him.

Girisha and his two sons lived in a single room in one of the slums behind the train station. His wife had died during Vijay's birth. The three of them spent very little time there, and Kumara was hopeful his father could start backing off his hours. He wondered whether it might be time to close the shop in the old city. They still did a good business there, but far less than they used to. The logistics of running it were getting complicated, especially since Geetha and Suresha moved out of the back alleys behind the shop.

Talk of licenses and permits kept resurfacing, both at the depot where they bought their supplies and with the middlemen who still controlled access to the suppliers. Kumara had a very hard time getting a consistent story from anyone. Every second time he went to buy inventory, the dealer would bring up the subject, vaguely suggesting that next time he had to show his license. Kumara always deflected, by now comfortable with their rehearsed lines, nodding his head and moving on. Bribing always succeeded in changing the subject, and he didn't worry too much about it. The last time he visited the drugs bazaar in the main market, he noticed that at least two shops were shuttered. When he inquired about the closure, one of the shopkeepers said that the old man had died, and no one in the family wanted to run the stall. The man shook his head, regretful over not being able to take it over himself, saying that they were getting less and less foot traffic in the drugs bazaar over the past year. More and more apothecary stalls and shops were opening on the various high streets and even back road bazaars.

Kumara smiled. He asked him about the rumors about licenses.

"Yes, I have heard about this. But only from those thieves who sell us the product. They can make up whatever story they want, and we have no way to know the truth."

"Have you tried to get any information from the government offices?"

"Why would I go to them for any information? This will just make me a target. No, no, I will just wait until something happens."

Kumara wondered just what that something might be. As he walked back home, he thought it might be worth talking with Geetha about the old city shop and what to do about it.

CHAPTER 17

Umesh was producing movies. After returning to Mysore, he longed for the company of the type of people he had met in Mumbai, so he enticed several writers and a few movie stars to come to Bangalore to make films in the local language. Starting after Independence, they had made several and were well on their way to putting Bangalore on the map of the new movie industry. He was very proud to have made the careers of two very popular film stars. One of them was a lovely young girl from Mysore. She reminded him of Noor.

Lathika was pregnant with their fourth child. His mother had died two years ago, probably from a heart attack; no one was quite sure. It had saved them from having to move.

Umesh hosted his colleagues routinely at his home for planning sessions. They would gather and talk well into the early morning hours about plots, music, and characters for their next film. At least twice a month, he would drive into Bangalore to check on movie sites, often staying over several days as important scenes and musical numbers were choreographed, rehearsed, and filmed. He had a driver, but occasionally he would drive himself, enjoying the feeling of being behind the wheel of his very own Rolls Royce.

The streets of Bangalore were very crowded. More and more people were coming into the city for work. Many factories his mentor, the Maharajah, had started in the twenties and thirties were still growing and drawing workers from around the countryside. Steel and iron works, paper mills, and chemical factories were all booming. At the same time, new industries were popping up, like telephones and transistors. The municipal government was on a spending spree, with huge road, rail, and public building projects underway. The number of cars had grown, and Umesh hardly ever went for a ride these days without passing several on the road. The last time he went out with his driver, they saw two funny-looking vehicles with three wheels chasing them down the road, honking their horns.

"What is this contraption?"

"Sir, I have seen a dozen of these in the last two weeks."

"It looks like a bicycle with a cart attached to the back."

"They are saying it is to transfer people around. The drivers of these are just like the rickshaw porters."

"It looks pretty dangerous to me. Do you know how much it costs to ride in one of these?"

"I don't know sir, but I believe there is a rule that they can only take two passengers."

Umesh laughed out loud. "I'm sure I saw at least four people in the last one that whizzed by us just now."

His driver smiled.

"Yes sir, you are correct. And now we must be careful when driving on the roads. They don't just belong to the automobiles anymore."

He sat back and looked out the window as his car made its way through the heaving main street and onto the outskirts of the city, where his latest film set was located.

• • •

Vijay was pedaling furiously, trying to get back to the Russell Market. He had been delayed at the old city shop, helping his father put a lot of new product away. He'd brought plastic bags full of yellow and green tablets on his bicycle and had to explain to his father that these were good for upset tummies. It was getting dark. Kumara and Geetha had compromised to open the old city shop only in the late afternoons and evenings since that tended to be when the inhabitants of the area were around. Many had moved out of the slums and into apartment blocks, but there were still some very poor day laborers who lived there and showed up at the end of the day after finishing their work.

Vijay pulled around a tuk-tuk and sped up on the straightaway. He was headed for the roundabout that would take him past Cubbon Park and onto the Russell Market. KR Circle was always busy. In addition to the autorickshaws and automobiles, there were trolleys and double-decker buses, not to mention the throngs of people walking through the roundabout. He screamed onto the roundabout assuming, as usual, that anything merging, whether human, animal or otherwise, would get out of his way.

The light from behind him cast his shadow on the road ahead. It was the last thing he saw before flying through the air and landing hard against the oncoming bus.

• • •

Umesh felt the car shudder and slow down. He looked up from his newspaper. His driver muttered something under his breath.

"What was that?"

"No problem, sir. It is nothing. Just something in the road. The car has driven over it."

Umesh looked out the window as his driver pulled out and circled around a bus that had stopped in the road. He could see a group of people standing around something on the ground.

"Did we hit someone?"

"Maybe sir, someone or maybe a dog, I am not sure. Do you wish that I stop?"

"No, no, but you should check the car later to make sure there is no damage. You know how long it takes to get anything repaired."

Umesh and his driver carried on around the roundabout on their way back to Mysore.

CHAPTER 18

Suresha finally decided to go home. He couldn't wait any longer. This had happened once or twice before. The boy might have been delayed for a variety of reasons, including an unforeseen errand for Kumara, or Geetha might have asked for a special side trip to get her something. He was keen on dinner and didn't even mention to Geetha that Vijay hadn't shown up at the shop.

Girisha was working in the old city shop. He usually got there late in the afternoon and closed the shop late in the evening. He didn't think twice that Vijay wasn't in their room when he returned. Normally, he would be at the Russell Market shop and wouldn't return until late at night.

Kumara closed his stall just before midnight. Lately, he had started to sleep in the shop to save himself the walk back and forth to his room in the short span of a few hours. Tonight, he decided to go home. He hadn't seen his father for several days and wanted to discuss the old city shop.

His father had fallen asleep sitting up, the remnants of his dhal and mudde dinner in his bowl. Kumara shook him gently.

"Hi, Appa. How are you doing?"

Girisha opened his eyes, not sure who had woken him.

"Ah, my son. I wasn't expecting you back tonight."

"I decided to come home. I want to discuss something with you."

He was still a bit dazed and sat up, rubbing his eyes.

"Vijay, Vijay!" he called out. "Can you bring me some water?"

Kumara looked around the dark room. He walked over to the corner where his brother usually slept. He poked at the bedclothes with his foot, trying to find his brother and nudge him awake.

"Appa, he is not here. Have you seen him today?"

"Yes, he was with me at the shop earlier on. We put a lot of things in order, and he made some labels for the pills so that we know what is what. He is a clever one, your brother. He was trying to help me remember the symbols for the different medicines," Girisha smiled.

"He must still be at the Russell Market then, or at least on his way home."

Kumara and his father chatted quietly about the business in the old city shop. They discussed whether it made sense to close it so that they could focus their time on the two most profitable shops. Girisha thought it was a good idea, but Suresha and Geetha would have to approve.

"I will go see them tomorrow after Vijay comes to the station in the morning. Uncle should be back home by the early afternoon." Kumara lay down and shut his eyes. He had a few hours to sleep before going back to the shop.

When the boy didn't turn up the next morning, Kumara didn't think much of it. He knew he would eventually get there. It was a very busy day, and he'd forgotten about the conversation he wanted to have with his uncle and aunt. By nightfall, though, he was starting to feel a bit annoyed. Where was he? His brother never missed a day at the train station. He wondered if Suresha or Geetha might be ill, and he had gone to their apartment to help with something. If Vijay was with them and he went there, he could see them all. He closed the shop just before midnight and started the journey towards the park.

KR Circle was about halfway to the park. Despite the late hour, it was busy with many people, ox carts, cows and quite a few bicycles. Kumara looked carefully at the faces, hoping to recognize his brother, finally on his way to see him. He continued, leaving the roundabout behind him, and made his way through the park.

He stepped over the sleeping old woman who was supposed to be the doorkeeper and walked up the stairs to the third floor. He turned the door handle and walked in. The rooms were quiet, and he could hear Suresha snoring in the back room. Geetha had heard him come in and was already lighting the candle.

"Ah Kumara, come in, come in," she waved him into the room.

"Hi Auntie, sorry to come so late."

"No matter, come, sit down."

"Auntie, have you seen Vijay?"

"I was going to ask you the same. He didn't come to the Russell Market the last two days. Suresha waited for him a long time but finally came home."

"He hasn't been to the train station either the last two days. My father saw him yesterday, but I don't know if he saw him today."

"Your brother is very reliable and serious. He doesn't stop on the way for games and gambling. Do you think someone stole him?"

"It's possible, but Vijay is getting around on his bicycle. He is too fast. When he was moving on foot, I warned him of these people who steal children off the street. He never had a problem."

"Maybe his bicycle got damaged, and he is getting it fixed somewhere?"

"It is possible. Perhaps we can look for him."

"Suresha and I will walk from KR Circle to the Russell Market. It's OK if we don't open the shop for one day. He may have broken down on this way there. But Kumara, I think you should look again from the roundabout to the station."

"I just came that way tonight. I didn't see anything."

"But you weren't looking for him along the road, right?"

"Well, no. I thought he was here with you."

"Well, you might see something if you walk a second time."

"You are right. Thank you, Auntie, for helping me."

"I hope we find him."

"Suresha, wake up. Kumara was just here. He says Vijay is missing."

Suresha had been in a deep sleep, and it took him several seconds to register what Geetha was saying.

"Kumara says he hasn't seen him for two days. We are going to try to find him tomorrow."

Neither of them could get back to sleep. At daybreak, they ate their breakfast in silence. Vijay was like a son to them. Around midday they left and walked through Cubbon Park toward the roundabout.

"You walk on that side of the road; I will walk on the other. And don't forget to ask the shopkeepers if they saw a young boy on a bicycle."

"But there are so many now. How will they remember just one boy?"

"Still, you should ask."

Suresha shook his head as he crossed over to the other side of the street.

Geetha walked up to the first kiosk on the corner of two roads that split off the circle. The young man sitting outside of the stall stood up as she approached. Like most shops along the road, he sold drinks, candy, cigarettes, umbrellas, and sunglasses.

"Madam, do you want a drink? I have water, Fanta, and Coca-Cola. What are you looking for?"

"Have you seen a boy on a bicycle the last few days?"

"Madam, I have seen many people on bicycles. Do you want a nice Fanta?"

"No, no, I am not thirsty. He was a young boy, twelve years old."

"No madam, I have not seen him. Is he your son?"

"No, he is my relative. I am sure you see many bicycles, but this was a young boy, not a man."

"Madam, no, I haven't seen anything." The young man had lost interest in Geetha as soon as he learned she wasn't a customer.

She moved on, looking for the next shop she might stop at. A few paces down, she passed a bigger one, one with three different minders guarding the displays of pots and pans hanging outside the shop.

"Have you seen a boy on a bicycle? He passes by here every day on his way to the Russell Market."

"Oh, Auntie, there are so many people passing on bicycles now. Has he run away from you?" The man was smiling.

"You are a stupid man. No, he hasn't run away. Have you been here every day?"

"Well, I have not been here for the last two days, but my colleague is here every day," he said as he motioned for his friend to come.

"This lady is looking for her son on a bicycle. How many bicycles have you seen here every day?"

The older man walked up to the pair, shuffling his sandals.

"I have seen many bicycles here every day. But almost every day there is an accident. There was a bicycle that hit a car a few days ago. I think it was a boy. He flew in the air and hit the bus. They have already taken the body away."

Geetha felt a wrench in her stomach. She had considered this possibility but avoided mentioning it to the others. She imagined that scenario to be much more likely than someone kidnapping Vijay.

"When did this happen?"

"Oh, I don't know. Maybe two or three days ago. It is happening a lot now, you know, with all the buses and now autorickshaws on the roads."

"What time was it, do you remember?"

"Maybe late in the afternoon. It was already getting a little dark. I saw the car that hit him. They must have pushed his bicycle very hard."

"What car?"

"It was a beautiful automobile. Like a festival cart. All silver and black."

She grabbed hold of the man's arm.

"Show me where this happened."

The man led the way a short distance from the shop. He stepped onto the circle, watching for the oncoming bus, and weaved his way through the ox carts and pedestrians.

"You see, the bus was coming from the other side, and the car from here. I didn't see it happen, but after, many of us came to look. The bus stopped, and the driver came down. But the boy was not moving."

"This must be the bus number 11, the one goes from the bus station to the trains?"

"Yes, I think so."

Geetha left the man standing in the road. She crossed over to where Suresha was.

"I think Vijay was hit by a bus. They are saying he is dead, but I am going to the bus station to see if I can find the driver. You must go to the hospital and find him."

Suresha's hands went up to his head in anguish. He started to wail. Geetha wasn't sure he could get there on his own, so she grabbed his arms and led him back to their apartment. He was sobbing and could barely walk.

"I am going to leave you here and go to the bus station. Please don't go outside. Just stay here until I return."

CHAPTER 19

On her way back down the stairs, she knocked on her neighbor's door. Nayla was quite a bit younger than Geetha. She had two boys and a daughter. They attended the local primary school and were on the morning shift. They were usually home after lunch, playing and wandering the streets.

"Geetha, hi, come on in. Are we going to the shops together later on?"

"No, sorry, not today. We are looking for Vijay. He is missing."

"No, what has happened?"

"We are not sure, but someone in KR Circle said they saw a boy on a bicycle get hit by a bus. They think he is dead. I am going to see if I can find out what happened, but I need to get a message to Kumara at the train station."

"Oh no, are you sure?"

"It sounds likely, but I hope it is not true. Can I send your son to Kumara to tell him what we discovered?"

"Yes, yes, of course. I think he is downstairs playing with his brother. Let's go find him."

The two women descended the stairs without speaking. Geetha was starting to lose her composure, overwhelmed by the reality that was setting in.

They found Nayla's eight-year-old son playing cricket with a gang of neighborhood children.

"Vivek, Vivek, come here. I need to speak to you."

The boy reluctantly left the game and walked over to his mother.

"You must go to the train station to Kumara's shop to give him a message."

"Oh, Mummy, but it's so far!"

"Don't argue with me. It is very important. Vijay may be dead. You know Vijay, Auntie Geetha's nephew?"

The boy shrugged. He had seen Vijay a few times but remembered him only because of his bicycle.

"Go to the apothecary shop at the station. It is the one with big red cross on the front. Kumara will be there. You must tell him that a boy on a bicycle has died near the KR Circle, hit by an automobile and a bus. Tell him I am going to the bus station to see if I can find something out."

The boy's eyes got bigger. The violence of the bicycle being hit by a car and a bus suddenly made his task urgent.

"Go, go, I will give you a rupee when you come back."

Geetha set off to the bus station.

It was a long way to walk, and she had a lot of time to think during the journey. What a misfortune. How would they manage now that there was one less person to work in the business? With no more sons to put to work, and Suresha and Girisha getting older, what would they do? Geetha remembered back to when her youngest son had died from cholera. Yes, she had been sad, but it was so commonplace to her that a child should die she had accepted it and moved on. Her husband had taken it much harder, and she secretly knew that he had hoped to have another child, but she had made every effort to ensure that would not happen. Now, it was too late.

Finally, she arrived at the bus station. It was late in the afternoon, and the bus would not have returned from its loop around the city. She walked up to the guard shack, hoping that someone would have some useful information. She wanted to find out what had happened, but there was not much more mystery for her. Vijay was gone; that was it. There was little upside to a broader story.

The booth was a dilapidated structure. It was barely big enough for one person to sit inside, with an opening that had no door but was covered with a beaded curtain. The smell from the open latrine opposite was very strong. It sent a wave of memory through Geetha.

The old man squatting on the floor outside the shack stood up as she approached.

"Do you want a ticket? Where are you going, Madam?"

"Listen, I don't want a ticket. I want to speak to the driver who was driving the bus two days ago."

The old man shook his head.

"We have many drivers. I can't remember who is driving when. What do you want with him anyway?"

"There was an accident. My nephew was hit by the bus two days ago. I want to know what happened."

"Auntie, it's not the driver's fault. There is no money. The drivers are poor. This happens almost every day now; someone gets in front of the bus."

"You stupid old man, do you think I want money? I am trying to find out for my family what has happened to our relative."

"Well, you will have to wait until the bus returns. Then you can ask the driver if he saw anything."

Geetha was not very hopeful. She guessed the driver would feign ignorance to ensure no repercussions would befall him. However, the mention of money made her wonder if he might be more forthcoming if she offered a few rupees.

"Fine, I will wait then."

•••

The little boy arrived at the shop. He looked dusty and tired, and Kumara nearly threw him out, given how many street beggars were around the shop.

"Geetha sent me," the child whispered, looking at Kumara warily.

"What do you mean Geetha sent you? How do you know her?" He grabbed the boy's arm and shook him.

"She sent me to tell you that Vijay is dead," he said, trying to shake out of Kumara's grip.

"What? She said this?"

"Yes, she said to tell you she is going to the bus station to look for the bus driver who hit him and that you must go to the hospital to find Vijay," and he started to sob, exhausted from the tension of his quest.

Kumara fell back a few steps, grabbing hold of the shop counter to steady himself.

"She said you would give me money if I came here to tell you," the boy gasped through his sobs, eyeing Kumara carefully.

He fished a couple of rupees out of his pocket to give to the boy.

"Here, here is your money. Do you want a drink? Coca-cola?"

A DANGEROUS TIME

The boy nodded as he pulled the notes gingerly from Kumara's hand.

Kumara was in a trance. He took a coke can from the shelf and handed it to the boy, who grabbed it and ran out of the shop.

How could Vijay be dead? It was impossible, he told himself. Geetha must be wrong. How could she know? He sat down on the stool behind the counter, holding onto his head, waiting for the wave of nausea to pass. He closed the shop and hurried to Victoria Hospital, the only place they would have taken Vijay. But he had to stop every few steps to hold onto something to prevent his knees from buckling. It took him a long time to get there.

CHAPTER 20

Geetha waited long into the night for the bus to return to the depot. She had no guarantee that the driver would be the one involved in the accident, but she had no choice. It was close to midnight when the bus finally pulled in.

"You, Driver, were you driving this bus a few days ago? Did you hit a boy on a bicycle? He is my nephew." Her tone was very strong. She wanted him to take her seriously. He was an older man, and she thought he would be kinder, more sympathetic.

"I have not hit anyone since a few weeks ago. It was, I think, Mano who was driving. He told me the boy hit the bus from the air."

"Mano. When is Mano coming here?"

"I think he is coming in the morning. The bus is starting after sunrise."

"What did he tell you about this?"

"He just told me maybe the boy was hit from behind because the bicycle did not hit the bus, just the boy. He said he saw the automobile driving away."

"What kind of automobile was it? Did he see it well?"

"Oh, I don't know. You will have to ask him." The driver was anxious to get away. He clearly felt sympathy, but knew he couldn't help her. Daily there were accidents on the road. Bad luck for her.

Geetha was tired and hungry. Now that she had to wait another few hours, she decided to walk down the road a bit to the food stalls that catered to the bus depot. She would find something to eat there before coming back. She did not want to miss Mano when he came to start his shift.

She crossed the main road in the dark, surprised at how many people were about. It was as if it was the middle of the day. She saw the row of shacks selling street food to the passersby. She carefully examined what was on offer, not liking the looks of any of the cooks, but everything smelled good to her; she was so hungry. Finally, she decided on some chapatis with a cup of egg curry. She sat on the ground alongside a group of day laborers to eat her meal. She had never been to this side of Bangalore. It seemed very cold to her, with big wide roads, mostly for the buses and automobiles, as if the city didn't want the pedestrians around. She could feel her eyes closing. The meal and the long day were making her sleepy. She got up, pulled her sari straight, and marched resolutely back toward the bus depot. She had only one chance to speak to this driver. She couldn't let herself fall asleep.

When Geetha returned to the bus depot, three buses were parked there, not just one. The others must have come in after she had gone to get her food. She was angry with herself. Maybe one of those drivers was the one, and now she would never find out. She walked back and forth in front of the buses to keep her sleepiness away. The old man in the shack eyed her suspiciously until he fell asleep. Finally, the light started to change, and she hoped the drivers would arrive soon.

Two men came from the road and approached the buses. Both were young, maybe her son's age. The hairs on the back of her neck stood up. She was sure these youths would not be happy to help her.

"Which one of you is called Mano?"

"Ah, it is me, Auntie. What do you want? Do you want a ticket?"

"No, no, I want to ask you about the boy who was hit in KR Circle a few days ago."

"Yes, you know, he flew through the air and hit the top of the bus with his head. It was a very loud noise. I came down from the bus to see, but everyone told me he was dead. I had to finish the route, so I had to go."

"Did you see the automobile that hit the boy?"

"Well, I didn't see the moment the car hit him, but I saw it drive away. I know this car. I have seen it many times in Bangalore. The owner is very famous. He is the maker of the movies shown at the cinema."

"Was it black with silver? I heard it was a very beautiful automobile."

"Yes, yes, a very nice Roseroyce. I know this car. The owner lives in Mysore, but he comes to Bangalore often. His name is Mr. NV. Everyone knows about him."

Geetha had never heard of him, but then, she never went to the cinema. It didn't matter. Now she knew where he lived. If he was that famous, everyone in Mysore would know where to find him.

"I am sorry, Auntie. Did you know this boy?"

She didn't answer and slowly turned away to start the journey home.

Geetha speculated on what to do next. Now that she knew who was responsible, what was it exactly that she wanted from him? Given the nature of the accident and the fact that the owner of the car was a very wealthy man with great status, she was sure he would care very little. He would not feel any guilt for taking the life of a boy, especially a low-caste boy. Geetha wondered if she wanted money for Vijay's death. Not really. Money was the last thing they needed. But why would he even give her money? She had no leverage at all.

She passed an apothecary shop, then again another one a bit further down the road and across the street. There were so many now, everyone selling drugs, medicines, powders, cosmetics. It wasn't like when they had started. She wondered, now that Vijay was gone, how would they cope with three stores, all the competition, and all the rumors about needing a license to sell the products, which she secretly worried about a lot. There was no way to get at the truth. None of them could read or write. They had no chance to get information from any authoritative source. All they were given was innuendo, lies, and greedy suppliers who wanted more and more bribes to sell them the same stuff they had been buying for years.

A rich man, an educated man, a man with status had killed Vijay. Maybe he could get them accurate information from the government. But why would he do this for her? He wouldn't; Geetha had no illusions. She had to find another way to scare him.

She passed by one of the many cinemas in Bangalore. She had never seen a movie, although Kumara had taken Vijay to see a few, and they would tell her all about the stories, the songs, and the dances. There was a long line of men waiting to enter the theater. She looked at the giant billboard showing a man and woman, arms intertwined, looking deeply into each other's eyes. She could just about read a couple of the words in the title in big letters. It seemed to be something to do with bees. She recognized this word because some local medicines were made with bee honey. It puzzled her to think a film could be about bees and lovers. Geetha smiled and chuckled to herself.

She remembered the story of a film that Kumara had told her, one about a wealthy landlord who is unkind and brutish toward his workers. The rich man was taken to jail at the end of the movie because of his callous and criminal behavior. It was very popular because it was a condemnation against the harsh treatment of lower caste people by the upper classes. Kumara had told her there was a lot of talk about this. Many protests were happening not only here in Bangalore but in many of the big cities far away. Geetha wondered whether a man who made such films could be threatened by someone claiming he had perpetrated the same cruelty on a low-caste boy. It was a stretch, she thought. The rich and privileged class always get what they want, and no one would dare to hold them to any standard of law or morality. But in this instance, she wondered if it might be worth it for him to negotiate with her. All she wanted was for him to obtain information about licenses from the authorities. She had no idea who these authorities were, but he might know if he was an educated man. Otherwise, she would tell him she would go to the theater and tell all the men standing in line about his crime. She shrugged her shoulders, cynical in her expectation that it would work, but she felt compelled to at least try.

Geetha finally arrived at her apartment. It was the middle of the day. Slowly, she climbed the stairs, bracing herself for Suresha's agony when she confirmed to him all the details of the tragedy.

PART V
GEETHA MEETS UMESH

CHAPTER 21

Kumara arrived at the constant mob of people and patients milling outside the hospital. He knew what to expect since he passed by the hospital daily on his way back and forth from his room to the train station. No matter the time of day, there was always a high level of activity outside the immense stone arches on the ground floor. He felt very light-headed, as if in a dream, as he asked one of the attendants outside for the location of the dead bodies brought in from the city.

"Go all the way around the building. You will see a separate small building; it is yellow. Go in there."

As he rounded the corner at the back end of the stately hospital, he saw a small and forlorn structure standing a good distance behind the main building. A man was squatting beside the open front door, smoking a cigarette.

"I am looking for my brother. I think he was hit by a bus in KR Circle."

At first, Kumara could only smell the smoke from the cigarette, but slowly, he caught the odor that emanated from the door. Kumara was used to strong smells around Bangalore, from the open latrines behind his room to the rotting fruit and flowers that would pile up at the sides of the streets before being hauled away by the poor street dwellers. But this was different. It closed up his throat, and he fell back a few steps, choking.

The man didn't budge but pointed him inside. Kumara was apprehensive to enter but had no choice.

The long corridor was dark, and he had to walk down the length of it before it opened up into a small room with several doors in the back. There was a desk, but no one was sitting at it. Kumara saw that one of the doors behind the desk was slightly open. Fighting back the tears from the combination of the smell and his emotions for Vijay, he went up to it and tried to call out, but he could only get a gasping croak out of his mouth.

"Is anyone there? I am looking for my brother."

Another long corridor went off to the left of the door. But it was dark, and he was afraid to walk down it.

"Hello?" he shouted, this time a bit more confidently.

As he squinted down the long hallway, he thought he could see a white figure moving towards him. Fear welled up inside him. He wondered what the apparition might be.

"I'm coming, I'm coming," the ghost said.

Kumara nearly turned to run but held his ground long enough to see the outline of the figure walking towards him. It was a man with no shirt and a long, dirty, and bloody apron wrapped around his waist.

"What do you want?" he asked in a harsh voice. "Why are you here?"

"I am looking for my brother," Kumara whispered.

"Speak up. I can't hear you."

Kumara cleared his throat and tried again.

"My brother was hit by a bus. I think he is here now."

"Where did this happen, do you know? I can only find the bodies inside if I know where they came from."

"It happened in KR Circle just two days ago."

"Two days? That's very fresh."

Kumara stared at him, blinking hard against the stench.

"You are lucky. Usually, after a few days, Krishnappa takes the bodies away to be cremated."

The man turned and walked back down the corridor. When he got halfway, he turned to see if Kumara was behind him.

"Come, come," he called out, flinging his arm out, beckoning him to follow.

They walked to the end of the hallway to a small room. Kumara's eyes were getting used to the dark and the smell. He saw several figures of different sizes on the floor, covered in dirty white shrouds.

"How old was your brother?"

"About twelve…"

The man scanned the bodies covered in sheets and approached the smallest one. He pulled the cover back, exposing Vijay's face and skinny shoulders.

"Is this him?"

Kumara collapsed onto the floor beside the body. He caressed Vijay's face and tousled his thick black hair as he'd done a million times.

The man stood back a few steps, giving him time and space for his grief.

"You can't pray for him here," he said eventually. "You have to either take him home or to the cremation ground. You have to pay Krishnappa to take him. But you have to pay me first."

"Who is Krishnappa?"

"He is the one who takes the bodies to be cremated. He can take your brother's body to your place if you want. He lives just out the back."

By the time Kumara and Krishnappa reached his room, his father had already left to open the city shop. He was relieved, since he was afraid of his reaction to the news. His brother had been much closer to their father these past few years. Vijay had cooked for the old man and taken care of him. While Kumara would see his brother almost daily, he only saw his father once every five or six days.

He settled Vijay's slight form on the floor in the center of the room and sat next to him for a long time, paralyzed by his grief. He was drained and vanquished from his quest and retrieval of his brother's body.

It's time to go, he told himself, there is a lot to do. First, he had to tell his father; then, he had to find Geetha and Suresha before arranging for the priest to come for the rituals. He shuffled along, hurrying on the one hand to get to the city shop but dragging his feet as well. He was mindful that his father was still happy, working in the shop, serving customers, oblivious to the news he was about to receive.

He drew a deep breath before walking up to the stall at the City Market. His father was sitting behind the counter, talking with a customer. His eyes lit up when he saw his son.

"Hey, Kumara, you are visiting me in the shop. You haven't been here in a long time."

"Yes, Appa, yes. I have something important to tell you."

"I am glad you are here. I have to get some more of those bottles for the coughing. I was going to tell Vijay to get me some, but I still haven't seen the rascal." Girisha smiled and winked.

Kumara didn't answer but waited until the customer paid and left.

"Father, Vijay is dead."

Girisha looked at Kumara as if he hadn't understood.

"Did you hear me, Appa? He is dead."

His father put his hand on his chest and started pounding.

"No, no, no!" he wailed.

Kumara grabbed his father's wrist to stop the blows. Girisha yanked his arm with force out of his son's grip and started to beat him on the head with his open hands.

"What are you saying? What are you saying? You don't know this, you don't know this!"

"Yes, it is true, I have his body. It is in our room."

Girisha stopped his assault and let out a long, croaking wail, which got weaker and weaker as the message sank in. He fell back into the stall, and Kumara was afraid he was going to die. He knelt and lifted his father's limp body to sit him up. He then reached on the shelf for the powder that had a strong smell, which he sold to many people for fainting, and held it under his nose. It took some time, but the old man eventually opened his eyes.

"Father, come. Can you stand up? I am going to take you home."

Girisha stared at his son with no comprehension.

Kumara lifted him, but his legs buckled. He closed up the stall, left his father inside, and went to find a porter. There weren't many about this time of day. He had to walk to the top of the street before finding one.

They loaded Girisha onto the cart, and Kumara followed them back to their room. He carried his father onto his bed and tried to give him some water. The old man was still in a fog, his mouth open, his eyes staring at his son with no sign of recognition. Kumara held him on his bed, rocking him slowly until his eyes closed, and he seemed to fall asleep.

It was by now quite late and Kumara left his father with Vijay to fetch his uncle and aunt. As he walked towards Cubbon Park, he had to cross KR Circle. He stopped and sat on some of the broken rubble on the side of the road. He imagined Vijay sitting there next to him, closed his eyes, and sobbed for a long time. He wiped his face and tried to stop crying, but when he saw the crowds, buses, cars, tuk-tuks, cows, and bicycles moving through the roundabout, even late at night, he wanted to shout: "Don't you know what has happened? Don't you know that Vijay is gone? You killed him!" But the words wouldn't leave his mouth. The hurt started to well up in his eyes once more.

He opened the door to the dark, quiet apartment. He wasn't sure anyone was there. But he soon saw Suresha's figure sleeping soundly on the mattress. Geetha wasn't there.

"Uncle, wake up." He shook him gently.

Suresha propped himself up and looked at his nephew, his eyes red and swollen from crying.

"Did you find him?"

"Yes, Uncle. I found his body; it is in my room."

Although Suresha expected this news, the sadness rose again, and he started to sob. Kumara put his arms around his uncle, trying to comfort him through his own tears.

"He was like a son to me...does my brother know?" Suddenly Suresha was mindful of Girisha's grief.

"Yes, Uncle, I told him, and it made him very ill. We must arrange for the priest and the cremation. Did Auntie Geetha really go to find the bus driver?"

"I don't know, Kumara. She left me here yesterday afternoon and I haven't seen her since. I will leave word with the neighbor for when she returns to come to your room for the ceremony."

The two men walked in silence back through KR Circle. They bought garlands, rice, a deepa, and some incense.

CHAPTER 22

"Your plan to go to Mysore to find the man who killed Vijay is a waste of time."

Suresha, Geetha, and Kumara were having a conference a few days after the cremation.

"I know who he is. He is making movies, and his name is Umesh NV."

"But what good is this? Do you think he will even admit to what he did?"

"All I can do is try. I will find him and tell him what a misfortune this is for us. I will ask him for money."

"Money is the last thing we need," Suresha wailed at her.

"Money is always needed," she snapped back. "Maybe this man can get us information."

"What information?"

"Information about all this talk of licenses. Maybe he can find out and tell us the truth."

"I don't think you will get this from him. He's going to tell you to get lost."

"I don't think so. We have enough money to go to the court. He won't want this."

Kumara had stayed quiet throughout this argument. During his grief, he had been thinking about the future of the three shops. His father, uncle, and aunt would be able to help for a while longer, but there was a big void coming, and if they wanted to keep the three shops open, they needed workers. Hiring outsiders was out of the question. No one could be trusted except family.

"We may have to eventually close the city shop," he said quietly.

"No, no, no, I am not closing any shops," Suresha fumed at him. "Prices are always going down, and if we close the shop we can't earn the same as we do now. And also, the city is growing all the time. All three of our shops are in the best locations, and we have a lot of customers. No, I won't accept this."

Geetha looked at the two men, thinking carefully before she spoke. She didn't want to close any shops either, and she was sure Kumara only said it because he saw no other path.

"Kumara, you are going to need some sons."

He looked up at her, a shy smile coming over his face.

"Auntie, you are always the clever one in this family. It is a nice plan, but first I need to find a bride! And even then, what if I only have daughters?"

"What about the dowry?" Suresha asked.

"The girl we will choose will come from a very poor family. They cannot afford a dowry."

"But who then will pay the brideprice?" Kumara asked. "I have no money."

"Don't worry, I will pay. We can make a very good price. But we must start immediately."

Geetha left for Mysore the very next day to find the man who killed Vijay. She would also see a couple of the matchmakers in town. She much preferred to find a girl from Mysore than Bangalore for Kumara. The girls were prettier and more delicate. So many people from the South had come to Bangalore to work, and she thought their children ugly.

She hadn't been back to Mysore since she and Suresha moved to Bangalore. That was before her sons were born, many, many years ago. Bangalore had changed a lot in that time, so she anticipated that Mysore would have also changed. She dressed in her best sari, pulled her hair into a tight bun at the bottom of her neck, and put some lipstick on. She needed to look her best for both her errands.

Geetha had a lot of time to think on the journey. She didn't know if she would be successful in shaming the driver and his rich boss into seeing her. She wanted to size up this man who made movies. He was sure to be well-connected. She thought if she could at least see him, she might have a chance to persuade him to help her. But it was just as likely the servants would throw her out. It was a gamble, but she had nothing to lose in trying.

She had discussed with Suresha about money for the girl. They had agreed on a sum she would offer as a brideprice for Kumara's wife. Kumara was a good catch, except for his withered arm. Many families would not want their daughter to marry such a man, but she had no intention of bringing it up with the matchmakers. Once the deal was done, she would bring the girl back to Bangalore and it would be too late by then for anyone to back out.

Geetha thought about her dead son and Vijay. Maybe she would take a few moments tomorrow, after she finished her mission, to stop in the temple and pray for them both, but also to pray for Kumara and his wife to have many sons. She would help the girl, as there were many herbs and seeds she could give her that would favor the conception of boys. Eventually, she fell asleep, rocked gently by the slow motion of the train heading for Mysore.

...

The three men left behind in Bangalore organized themselves to man the shops in this new paradigm. The biggest headache was communication. Now that they had lost their runner, getting messages to each other was a real challenge. Kumara told his father that he would come back to their room once every few days to see him. And since Suresha's apartment was much closer to the station than the Russell Market, he would do the same and go there for planning and logistics. And despite serious misgivings, he decided to get a bicycle for himself, to speed up all the back-and-forth travel.

Kumara was nervous. He had never really thought about getting married. The shops took up all his time, and he was a bit shy about his arm. The day Geetha left for Mysore, he suddenly was mindful of the girls and women walking on the streets and coming into his shop. He analyzed their faces, their clothing, the way they walked, and whether they smiled or frowned. He paid attention to how they spoke to him when asking for their medicines; some had sweet voices, and some were harsh. He noticed their figures and their hair, and wondered what Geetha would come back with. She had promised him she would explain what he had to do to make his wife happy. She told him it wasn't that hard. Kumara's anxiety was tempered with excitement, and he went about his daily business with a spring in his step and a new sense of anticipation and energy.

• • •

Geetha wondered if the matchmaker she planned to see was still around and in business. She must be pretty old by now. It was the best place to start. She set off from the train station, remembering her way quite easily. Mysore had changed, but it was still a beautiful place. There were more people than when she had left but far fewer than the crowds in Bangalore. She turned into the alley and found the doorway she was looking for.

A beaded curtain hung over the opening, and she stood outside and called out.

"Good morning. Is the matchmaker Lakshmi still living here?"

A small child poked her head out of the beads.

"My mother sent me to tell you Lakshmi is dead."

"Who is taking over from her? I need to see the matchmaker."

The child turned to hear what was being said from inside the room. There was an exchange between her and her mother, most likely describing Geetha so her desirability as a customer could be assessed.

The child beckoned her to enter.

It was the same room she remembered from many years ago when she had been brought here by her mother and handed over to Suresha's. It was a small room with an old mattress in the corner and a few cushions strewn around. The faded, dirty picture of Parvati hanging from the wall flooded her with memories. She smiled and sat on the floor before the child's mother.

"I was one of your mother's matches many years ago. I live in Bangalore now, and my nephew needs a bride."

"Yes, my mother died many years ago. I am doing the business now."

"Our family is prepared to make a brideprice. I want a girl that is ready to go now. One that is ready for children. I want a healthy one who comes from a big family. I need a lot of babies."

The matchmaker smiled.

"You are very wise to offer a brideprice. Dowry is impossible for some of my clients, but they have many good girls. It is a waste. They will never marry because they cannot afford a dowry. They will end up on the streets or sold to the brothels."

"Yes, I think it is simpler, and fewer politics with the family, eh?" Geetha winked at the woman, who laughed.

"Yes, yes. I have at least three girls you can choose from. Let me tell you about them, and we can go and see them. Then we can discuss the price."

CHAPTER 23

Umesh was trying to decide whether to go to Bangalore today or tomorrow. He had to spend several days there finalizing the production finances for his latest movie. It was getting late, and he didn't like driving the car in the dark such a long way. They already had a dent in the front where they had hit something in the road. He pulled his pocket watch out; it was five o'clock. If they left now, they might get there by midnight. It would most likely be too late to see his mistress; she wouldn't be expecting him. It wasn't worth it. He would go tomorrow morning and call ahead on the telephone. He told his servant to let his wife know he would have a meal with her and the children tonight.

• • •

Geetha and the matchmaker started out to visit the three prospects. They walked through the town to the outskirts, where many of the poor lived with their families. The matchmaker had sent word ahead so the girls were called back from working in the fields.

They walked down a road lined with hovels made of bamboo and mud, with dried grass covering the roofs. Geetha herself used to live along this row, somewhere further down, until she married Suresha, and they moved to Bangalore. Nothing much had changed here.

The matchmaker walked up to one of the huts and called from outside.

"It is me. Send the girl out to me so we can have a look."

A man came out, followed by a young girl. He wore the loincloth of the farm workers, was barefoot, and had his head wrapped in a dirty turban. He smiled at the matchmaker, showing three of his front teeth missing. He pushed the girl out in front of him.

"Ah, this is Anupama. She is a good girl. Strong. She can cook and works very hard."

The girl was very skinny, but this was to be expected. These families would barely have food to eat, and the girls would be fed after the men and boys. She was covered with a long shawl that probably belonged to her mother. Geetha walked up and pulled it off her head.

"Can you sing something for me, child?" The girl's voice wobbled a bit. She was nervous.

"OK, that's enough. Open your mouth." The girl had most of her teeth.

She examined each hand, front and back, making sure she had all her fingers.

"Take off your clothing."

Without any hesitation, the girl let her shawl drop to the ground. She walked around the girl, inspecting a couple of birthmarks and checking under her arms. She also checked her head to see what might be living in her hair. She asked the girl to walk back and forth, eyeing her carefully for any sign of a limp.

"Are you her father? How many children do you have?"

"I am her father. I have three sons and two daughters."

"Are they all still living?"

"My first son died before he was walking. All the others are still here."

Geetha motioned to the girl that she could dress. She turned to the matchmaker and said she was ready to see the next one.

"This is the best one I think," the matchmaker said in a low voice as they continued along the row.

She was right. The other two girls would be a lot less money. One had a club foot, and the other was blind in one eye. The two women moved off to sit under a tree to discuss business. Geetha wanted to be sure the girl was already menstruating. She stressed she didn't have time to buy a child bride and wait two years before she would get pregnant. The matchmaker assured her that it was the case. She said she had confirmed it herself. They haggled a little bit, not too much, and soon reached an agreement. She told the matchmaker her family would return to Mysore in a week or so for the marriage.

"Do you know about the man Umesh NV? He lives in Mysore. He is making movies, I hear."

"I know about him. He lives in a very big house in the area behind the palace. If you ask anyone they can tell you which one."

Geetha took her leave and headed back into town to find the man who killed Vijay.

As she walked through the streets, a lot of memories came to her. She thought about her mother and her father whom she had not seen since she left. For sure they were no longer living. She thought about her two brothers, both of whom had died when they were small, and her older sister who had left to be married before her. She tried to remember her sister's face, but couldn't see the features in her mind.

She reached Umesh's home just after dark. She went around the back, where a large stable stood across the courtyard. This is where they probably keep the car that hit Vijay, she thought to herself. Sure enough, through the window, she saw the sleek black Rolls Royce with the silver shiny trim parked to one side. Seeing no one about, she went towards the house to the entrance for the servants and deliveries.

Geetha walked right in. There was a wooden table, and three men were sitting around it having a meal.

"I am looking for the driver."

"I am the driver. I am Vivek. What do you want?"

The man who answered was young, with a small mustache and short hair. He looked very tidy and was dressed in long English-style trousers and a white shirt with a collar.

Geetha looked the part as well, in her mustard gold sari, with proper leather sandals and a handbag.

"You are the driver of the Rolls Royce that hit a boy on a bicycle in Bangalore, near KR Circle."

"Who are you? How do you know this?"

"I am the boy's aunt. I know because many people saw the automobile. It was the automobile in the stable in the back."

"Listen, he wasn't paying attention and wasn't looking where he was going. I didn't even see him. I just heard something bump the car in the front."

"Well, you killed him. He is dead. Now we have no one to work in our shops. We are going to have to close them because Vijay is dead and my husband is getting old. You have taken away our livelihood. This is a great misfortune for us."

"Lady, it's not my problem. You have no reason to come here begging for money. Go on, get out of here."

"Yes, it is a problem for you. I am going to stay here every day until I see your boss. Then I will tell him what has happened and that you didn't even stop to see what you had done."

"You are crazy," he smirked. "He doesn't care about your problems."

"Listen, I know he is making films. He is coming to Bangalore a lot. I can make a lot of trouble for him. I will stand outside the movie house and tell everyone how he killed a young child with no remorse. You will see. People will be angry with him."

The young man smiled.

"You think anyone will care about that? Everyone is waiting for the new movies to come. You think they will leave because of this? Impossible!" and he laughed.

"You are wrong. I will come here every day until I see him."

"Yes, you can come here every day, but no one will let you see him," the driver retorted and stormed out of the kitchen, his meal half-finished.

The other two men had quietly watched the scene. They were both older and grayer, and one had a patch over his left eye. One of them stood and addressed Geetha.

"I will see the boss and let him know about your sorrow. He is a good man, and he will be kind to you. This young man is very proud. He thinks too much of himself just because he is driving an automobile."

"Thank you, you are very good to me. Have you worked here long?"

"Since I was born. I have known the boss for many years. I will ask him."

"Is he here tonight?"

"Yes, you are fortunate. I think he will return to Bangalore tomorrow. Come, Sister, sit here. I will bring you some food."

Geetha was quite grateful to sit for the first time all day. And she was very hungry.

"Thank you, thank you. Yes, I am very tired from my journey."

"I will be seeing him in a little while. I will explain to him that you are here and that you would like to speak to him."

She nodded to the man.

"Are you going to ask him for money?"

"Yes, but I also want to ask if he can help us to get some information from the government."

"Oh, that will be most interesting to him. He will be curious; he is most unhappy all the time with the government," the man smiled.

Geetha ate her dhal and curd slowly, feeling somewhat hopeful that the man she had come to see might be willing to help. The old man seemed to know him well enough that she cautiously trusted his words.

"What is your name, Brother?"

"I am Sanjay. And what is your name?"

"Geetha, Geetha Ravindran. I was born here in Mysore but have been living in Bangalore for a long time."

He told her to wait in the kitchen. If his boss agreed to see her, they would come together to talk to her.

CHAPTER 24

Sanjay rose from the table and slowly shuffled off. Every night, after the family ate their dinner, he would go to see his master in his study to get any special instructions, to discuss any matters regarding the house, and to update him on any issues. While their roles were master and servant, they had developed a familiar rapport. Every night, they exchanged gossip and talked about events around Mysore. Umesh always confided in Sanjay what he was up to when he went to Bangalore.

"Mr. Umesh, how are you this evening?"

"Good, Sanjay, good. I decided to go to Bangalore tomorrow, so can you let Vivek know? I want to leave in the morning."

"Yes, of course, I will attend to it."

"I am sure Lathika will discuss it with you, but we are inviting some guests to the house for the festival. She will let you know what to prepare. I will be back from Bangalore by then."

"Yes, Mr. Umesh. Mr. Umesh, a woman has come here from Bangalore to see you."

"Really? Who is she? What does she want?"

"It seems that when you were in Bangalore some days ago, Vivek hit her nephew with the car, and he is now dead."

"Ah, please, Sanjay. How does she know it was my car? Do you know how many people are being hit by vehicles nowadays? It could have been anyone."

"Well sir, it seems she is sure that our car was involved. She is a well-dressed, clean woman who speaks well. She has shoes and a handbag. She is not some beggar from the streets. She is not untouchable."

"I can't help it if Vivek doesn't watch where he is going. He never told me about this."

"Vivek always thinks he is better than the rest of us. He is very proud to be your driver. He thinks he has a special place because of this."

"Well, he doesn't. But it is hard to find drivers. What does she want? Money?"

"It seems, yes, but she wants to meet you to ask you for something."

"What? I don't want to see some woman who comes here making accusations."

"She told me that she wants information from the government. She thinks that you can help her due to your station."

Umesh was suddenly intrigued. A woman from Bangalore wants information from the government. Maybe she was just trying to help someone get into a university or college and needed the connections he might have. The fact that Sanjay was asking him to meet her carried some weight for him.

"Alright then, let's go see this woman of yours."

When they arrived at the kitchen, Geetha had finished her supper and cleared her plate away. She did not want to meet such a brahmin with dirty plates on the table. She stood up when they walked in.

"Geethamma, this is my boss, Mr. Umesh. He has kindly agreed to see you and to offer his prayers for your nephew's soul."

"I am very grateful for this. The loss of my nephew is a big misfortune for my family. We are running three shops in Bangalore, and Vijay was the future of our business. My husband and I are getting old, and we had no one but Vijay to continue our work." She saw no reason to mention Kumara.

"I am sad for you, but what can I do? I can't help you with your business."

"Well, I think I will ask you. We sell all kinds of products to help with pain, blisters, headaches, and other problems. Every month, new miracles are coming to Bangalore, and we sell them to our customers. But we have heard many rumors lately about the government asking for licenses to sell the products. We don't know if people are telling us the truth or just lying for more bribes. My family is not educated. We have no way to find out the truth."

"So you sell medicines to help people?"

"Yes, we have been in this business now for many years, and it has been very lucky for us. We were doing a good business, but now that Vijay is dead, if we can't find out the facts about the licenses, our future is in big trouble. You understand what the situation is you have put us in."

"You know, I am actually a pharmacist."

Geetha looked blankly at Umesh. She had no idea what that meant.

"I have been to the university in Varanasi to study how drugs are made and how they can cure people."

She studied Umesh carefully. This revelation was astonishing to her. She wondered if he was lying.

"I thought you were making movies. This is what they told me in Bangalore."

"I do make movies now, but many years ago this is what I studied. I think I can help you."

Geetha and Umesh made a deal. He agreed to get information about upcoming rules and regulations and send his driver to see her when he came to Bangalore. He suggested that she could pass any messages on to Vivek if she had any further inquiries that might give her an advantage.

"I am sad about your nephew. I hope you can keep your business despite this misfortune."

Umesh gave her some money. She looked at the bills. Her memory flashed to the day, many years ago, when she had looked at similar money after Suresha had come home from his accident with the Maharajah's car. This time, there were only three bills, each with the symbol "100". Well, she thought to herself, after all, he's not a maharajah.

Geetha walked out into the night, pleased with what she had accomplished that day.

Umesh went up to bed and decided to sleep in his wife's room. He needed to talk about the events of the evening. His romantic side was stirred by Geetha's story, and the coincidence of their shared exposure to the drug trade had caught his imagination.

"I wonder if we can make a movie script with this story."

Lathika laughed out loud.

"You just met a clever low-caste woman, and now you want to make a movie about her. No one is interested in people like this."

"No, Lathika, you are wrong. There is a lot of talk these days about giving the Parayas and Shudras more rights, education, and jobs. It is a very big political discussion. Nehru is always making speeches about this. It could be a very popular film."

Lathika had already rolled over to go to sleep. She liked all the movies her husband made, although some were a bit too moralistic for her. She much preferred the happy ones, with lots of songs and dancing.

• • •

Geetha lay down on the floor in the matchmaker's room. She, too, was struck by the coincidence of their involvement in the drug trade, even though he was not actively engaged in it. She felt sure this fact made him more agreeable to her request. She knew at the start that her mission was a long shot, and she was lucky that the old servant had liked her. Otherwise, she would have been thrown out into the street. She fell asleep quickly, worn out by the day's successes.

CHAPTER 25

Geetha arrived home the next day to find Suresha in a state.

"It's good that you got back so quickly. We have a big problem. This man bought some medicine for his baby, and it has died. He was at the shop today shouting at me and threatening me."

"What does that have to do with us? Babies are dying all the time."

"He says I sold him the wrong medicine. He says I killed his baby."

"Did he leave?"

"Only after telling me he is going to go to the police."

"Ah, now that we don't have the British anymore, people are suddenly so brave to accuse."

"I think he wants money."

"We can't just give him money. If people find out we are giving money to our customers, everyone will be there claiming that we sold them something wrong. Tell me what happened."

"Did you see the man who killed Vijay? Did you bring a bride for Kumara?"

"Yes, yes, I had a good day in Mysore. But tell me what happened first."

"Well, the morning you left for Mysore, I went to the shop as usual. A man came in—"

"Was he young? Old? How did he look?"

"He was young, maybe a bit older than Kumara. He was just a laborer. He said his baby was crying all the time, and what did I have to calm it down? I asked how many days it had been doing this, and he told me just two."

"Did you tell him to take the baby to the doctor?"

"That is just what I told him. He said he didn't have money to go to the doctor. I asked him if the baby had liquid excrement, and he said he didn't know."

Geetha made a snort.

"So I told him I could sell him the opium for babies. I think it is called "Anodyne." But I said he must be careful not to give the baby too much. I told him a small bottle is only three rupees. And can you believe it, he starts to bargain with me."

"So I sold it to him for two rupees and a half, and he left. Then, this morning, he was back at the shop shouting that I killed his baby."

"That baby was going to die anyway. It has nothing to do with us."

"Wait, it's even worse. I asked how much he gave the baby. He said half the bottle, then later the other half because it made the baby quiet, and then it fell asleep. I told him he killed the baby himself, not me!"

"So he gave the baby the whole bottle?"

"Seems to be he did. But I think you are right. If the baby was already sick for two days, maybe it was too late."

"I am sure. Do you think he will come back?"

"I don't know. No one has ever come to tell us about a dead baby before."

"That doesn't mean there weren't any. Babies get sick and die all the time. I think it is all these young foreigners coming to Bangalore. Now that we have our own courts and government, they think they can sue and blame everyone else for their misfortunes."

"What should I do if he returns tomorrow?"

"I think if he returns, you should just tell him to go away. His baby was going to die anyway."

"What if he goes to the police?"

"I don't think the police will take this accusation seriously. And even if they do come to the shop, you just tell them that it was the father's fault the baby died, not yours."

Suresha felt a bit more confident after talking the situation through with Geetha. She was right, it was absurd to think that he was responsible.

"So tell me about your trip? Was Mysore changed much?"

"Not much, but many more people than when we left. I found a girl for Kumara. Hopefully, she will be a good wife. We will find out."

"What about Vijay? Did you find the man with the car?"

"Yes, and I was very fortunate. I met him at his house. He is going to help us find out the truth about all this talk of licenses. He knows a little about our business. He said he studied how to make drugs and medicines in university."

"So he is a doctor?"

"Not a doctor, but one who knows how medicines work. He said he worked for the government in Delhi for a time."

Suresha patted her on the shoulder.

"You had a very good trip. I am glad you are back home." He had missed his wife during her two-day absence.

"We will all go to Mysore in a few days for the wedding. I will buy a red sari and a Thali necklace for the girl. We will attend a mass marriage ceremony at the temple. It is all arranged."

Even though she was exhausted, Geetha found it hard to fall asleep that night. Vijay, Kumara, Anupama, Suresha, roseroyces, and dead babies were all competing for space in her thoughts. Even her son was there in the background. He had taken a job teaching at a school north of Bangalore, and she hardly saw him anymore. No matter. She had to take care of Kumara and his new wife now. She was sure that not so far in the future, both her husband and his brother would be gone. She just needed enough time to see Kumara take over the shops. As she finally dozed off, her last thoughts were of Anupama and the babies she hoped would come.

CHAPTER 26

Kumara met his wife-to-be for the first time at the ceremony. Many couples were married in the temple that day. It was like being at a festival. Kumara was happy and nervous at the same time.

"Auntie, she is beautiful!" He was beaming.

"Well, she is OK. She has all her fingers and toes, both eyes and ears. She will do."

Anupama smiled shyly, relieved that Kumara was quite young. Her mother had warned her of the possibility that she could be marrying an old man, that he might beat her, that he might pimp her out to his friends, or that he might even abandon her. At least the first of these worries was laid to rest. As for the remaining, time would tell.

That night, Anupama and Kumara slept in the same bed with a bamboo pole between them, forbidden to consummate the marriage, much to their mutual relief.

The day after the wedding, the family returned to Bangalore. Anupama was dazzled by everything she saw.

The train scared her. It was like a living thing, breathing steam and screaming as it slowed down to stop at the platform. She was fascinated by all the people, their colorful clothing, and the frantic level of activity.

Geetha spoke softly to the girl on the journey back. She described their business and the three shops, carefully avoiding making it sound like they were very successful. She hoped the girl was bright enough to learn to read, maybe even write. Over the years, Geetha had taught herself to recognize the English and German characters printed on the medicine boxes and packaging to at least differentiate the names of the medications they were selling. She would start teaching the girl immediately. She would also go to the old drugs bazaar to get the seeds and powders to help the girl have boy babies. Geetha knew of these, but having never used them herself, she could not be certain if they would work. Chances were good, though, she thought, since Suresha, Girisha, and even Bina had only ever had boy children.

"Auntie, I am going to the shop at the station for a few hours," Kumara said.

"Well then, Suresha and I will come with you to the shop for a few minutes before we go home."

When they disembarked the train, they all walked over to the stall. Girisha embraced his new daughter-in-law and went off to rest in his room.

"I will come back in a few days to spend some time with Anupama. I think we will call you Anu. It is a nice name. I will teach you to read the labels and the names of the different drugs."

"Go on Auntie, you and Uncle must be very tired after the journey."

"Yes, we are. But Kumara, you must start tonight with Anu. There is no time to waste!"

Kumara turned red, stealing a sideways look at his wife. "Don't worry, Auntie, don't worry…"

Geetha smiled and turned with Suresha to leave.

Anu had stood quietly throughout this exchange. She realized that Geetha was going to leave her with Kumara, and all the events of the last twenty-four hours and the unknowns of the next took over, and she started to sob uncontrollably.

Kumara saw her crying and panicked. He couldn't run after Geetha; she was already gone. He suddenly remembered Vijay doing the same thing for a long-forgotten reason many years ago. He instinctively went to her, put his arm around her shoulder, and just stood there. After all, she was probably the same age as Vijay, he thought. They stood there together for a long time until the sobs subsided into shorter and shorter heaves, and the overwhelming feelings passed. She looked up at Kumara, her eyes red and her cheeks wet from her tears. Kumara bent over and gently brushed his lips against hers. He sat her down on the floor of the shop behind the counter until later in the night, when he decided it was time to lock up and go home.

The girl hadn't said anything to Kumara since they had arrived. Now, as they walked slowly back towards Kumara's room, she spoke.

"I'm hungry."

Kumara smiled. "Well of course you are. Stupid me, I should have thought about this. Here, we can stop at some of the stalls on the way. I will buy you some food."

Kumara bought some chapatis from one vendor and some dhal from another. They sat on the ground, sharing their first meal. Anu tried to smile at him, her mouth full.

"Thank you," she said, barely able to talk.

"You were really hungry I see," Kumara answered, not sure what to say next. "You must also be very tired. Come, we are almost home."

They walked the rest of the way in silence. It was almost midnight when they arrived at Kumara's room. His father was fast asleep in his corner. Kumara showed Anu his mattress in the opposite corner of the room.

"We will sleep here together tonight. I will soon get a bigger mattress so we can have more space."

With that, he got down and squeezed himself to one side of the mattress. He patted the space next to him, signaling her to come.

"Come lie down. Just go to sleep. This is your home now. Don't worry."

Anu hesitated for a few seconds, apprehensive but resigned to what would come next. But as soon as she lay down, Kumara rolled over with his back towards her. Relieved, she closed her eyes, the events of the day swirling around her head, and she was soon asleep. Kumara listened for her breath to steady, and he turned around. Laying on his side, Kumara watched her for a long time. He was much too excited to sleep. But he didn't touch her that first night, a little out of fear, a little out of respect, and a little out of pity.

PART VI
UMESH HELPS GEETHA

CHAPTER 27

Umesh set about to keep his promise to Geetha. He hoped to find some of the papers from his brief stay in Delhi when he had worked on the Drugs Commission.

"Sanjay, do you know where my papers are from when I returned to Mysore?"

"I think they are put away in the little room at the back of the kitchen. No one has looked in this place for many years." Sanjay had a wry smile on. "I had asked you before to throw them away, but you wouldn't let me."

"Well, I thought it would be wise to save them. One never knows when one will need influence or some connection to someone in Delhi," Umesh smiled back.

"Of course, sir, that is why we have kept them all safe. But I cannot find the information for you. You will have to look yourself."

"Yes of course Sanjay, I understand." He was careful not to embarrass Sanjay, who had never learned to read. He knew this was a matter of regret for him.

Umesh stood back and looked at all the containers and shelves loaded up with his belongings from so many years ago. He scratched his head, not knowing really where to start. In the far corner, he found several sacks full of clothing and shoes that clearly didn't fit him anymore. Ah, he thought, I was a trim and dapper young man in those days. He rummaged through a few of the bins repurposed from food storage and found some binders and bundles of papers that looked like they might be from the right vintage. He untied one of the packets and everything fell apart onto the floor. He cursed and knelt down to collect them, and there, in the middle of the folded letters, notebooks, and envelopes, was a photo. It was a picture of Noor, taken during their last days in Mumbai together. He smiled, studying it for a long time. He wondered what she was up to, whether her marriage had been a good one, and if she had many children. He pushed the photo back into the pile, realising this wasn't the bundle he was looking for.

Finally, he located the notebook and letters that he had in mind. He stared at them, reflecting on how bored and impatient he had been with that whole process. He had no regrets about leaving it all behind. Making movies was much more rewarding.

Umesh took the papers back to his study and opened them up on his desk. His clear, strong handwriting was all over the notebook. He sifted through them, looking for the names of the different members of the Commission, trying to remember the faces and personalities of the people he'd worked with so long ago.

The first name he came across was Professor Pradesh. He thought for a moment, trying to picture him and what his relevance was. He remembered him as a fidgety old man with thick glasses who was always embarrassed to speak when they met. He didn't think he was the right one to approach for his mission. The next name was Dr. Gupta. This one might be better, he thought. Dr. Gupta was the Chairman of the Commission. He was a fat man whose tunic buttons always bulged out over the top of his large belly. A lifelong bureaucrat, he had carefully steered the Commission away from any quick and efficient decisions, making sure he maximized the amount of time in between meetings so that the project timeline dragged on for years. This was why Umesh had tired of the work and given up. Surely, the doctor would still be there helping the government to bring legitimacy and order to the drug trade in India.

Umesh wrote a letter to Dr. Gupta, reminding him of his work as a young man on the Drugs Commission. He explained his desire to perhaps open a pharmacy in Mysore and Bangalore. He asked for information on what formalities the Commission had prescribed for the licensing of such an endeavor. He closed by extolling the virtues and extreme importance of Dr. Gupta and emphasized his grand and most important position in the government. There, he thought, that should do the trick.

The letter was mailed to Delhi. It would take about a month for it to arrive and perhaps a month or more for the good doctor to reply. Things moved very slowly in the halls of government, especially in Delhi. That was all he could do for now.

...

Despite Geetha secretly feeding Anu many different powders that were supposed to favor the conception of boys, her firstborn had been a girl. Undeterred, she doubled down on her treatment with more potions to hurry along the next pregnancy. When the baby died, Geetha gave all the right sentiments of sadness, but in her heart, she thought it wouldn't hurt to have one less mouth to feed, especially since the girl was clearly pregnant again.

Anu was showing great promise in her ability to identify and reproduce labels for the many different drugs they were buying and selling. Kumara bought pills in bulk, and she would fill little bags with a few each and label them according to the ailment they were intended to cure. Sometimes she got things mixed up, but no matter, it all went to the shops and was quickly sold. All their customers consistently returned for more and more.

Girisha's health was going downhill. Even though he was younger than Suresha, after Vijay's death, he seemed to succumb to a mysterious illness that made him forgetful and tired. He was listless and made many mistakes handling money at the shop. Anu, who was with the old man the most, told Kumara that his father was sleeping a lot, and she could hear him shiver in the night. They tried to give him some of the medicines they sold that purported to give life and vitality, but nothing worked.

Anu woke up one morning and started sorting out the inventory Kumara had brought to the room several days ago. She had to weigh and package a lot of pills. Her husband would be back soon to pick them up.

She always let her father-in-law sleep until later in the morning. She went to wake him up with some porridge she made on her chulha. He was still asleep, with his mouth open. Anu shook him gently.

"Good morning, Appa."

Girisha didn't respond.

"Appa, wake up. I have made you some ragi ganji." She shook him a bit more firmly and felt his hand; it was cold.

She pulled back, afraid, unsure what to do. She thought she should go get Kumara, but then she couldn't leave all the merchandise unattended in their room. She started to cry. Girisha had been kind to her. He told her funny stories, and they'd shared many meals together. He had made her feel accepted and welcome in their family. When she suddenly realized he would no longer be there, the void of his loss overcame her and her knees buckled. She sat on the floor near his body for a long time, sobbing gently.

Later that morning, Geetha came to Anu's room. She knew the baby was due any day now and hoped to be there when it was born.

"Ah, Auntie, I am glad you are here. Father has died in the night."

"Let me see him."

"He is there in the corner, where he normally sleeps."

Geetha knelt by the Girisha and felt his hand. It was ice cold.

"Has Kumara been here? Does he know?"

"No, Auntie, he hasn't been here for a few days, so I think he should come soon."

Geetha's main concern was for the baby that was coming. She couldn't risk Anu giving birth in the same room where Girisha's body was kept. So she brought her to the neighbor's room, telling the old woman who lived there with her son, daughter-in-law, and their three children that she would get word to the midwife to check in on Anu while she went to give the news to Kumara and Suresha.

Geetha went to the station first. She knew Kumara would be surprised to see her. The shop was crowded with people buying their supplies before boarding the trains. She walked right up to the counter, pushing through the mob of customers.

When Kumara saw her, his first thought was that the baby had come. He smiled at Geetha.

"Ha, Auntie, you come here so rarely. You must have news for me!"

"Yes Kumara, but it is sad news I bring you today. Your father has died."

The words didn't register at first. The smile faded from his face, and a coldness came over him. His father had become so weak and frail since Vijay's death, and he had expected this day to come eventually. But its arrival made his stomach twinge and churn, and tears filled his eyes.

"Come," Geetha said softly. "You must close the shop and bring the priest to your room."

Kumara was in a trance. Geetha turned to the crowd waiting to be served.

"Go, we are closing this stall. Our relative has died. You must go somewhere else to buy your needs."

The crowd fell silent and slowly dispersed. Geetha helped Kumara, still paralyzed by his grief, draw the metal roll-down shutter, and they left.

"Your father was crushed by Vijay's death. This is what killed him."

"You are right, Auntie. That driver has killed two of our family, not just one."

"I have left Anu with your neighbor. I will go to the Russell Market and bring Suresha to your room."

Geetha's sober attention to the logistics brought Kumara back from his despondence.

"Yes, I will go now. Thank you, Auntie, for being such a good mother to us."

Geetha hurried off on her own errand to tell Suresha about his dead brother. She was wary that this blow, on the heels of Vijay's death, would be very hard on him.

A DANGEROUS TIME

When she arrived in the late afternoon, things were quiet at the Russell Market. She walked into the empty shop and saw Suresha dozing at the counter. He is getting old, she thought before waking him.

"Suresha, wake up! You can't fall asleep like this in your shop. Those little street beggars will come and steal your merchandise!"

"Ah, Geetha, what are you doing here? Has the baby come?"

"I have sad news. Your brother has died. You must close the shop and go to his room."

Suresha stood from his chair and let out a long wail, his hands raised to either side of his head.

Geetha tried to comfort him. "Come, come, we must go and pray over him."

But Suresha stumbled backward, nearly falling on the floor. Geetha thought they should wait a bit before setting out to make sure he found his composure and his footing.

They reached Kumara's room just as the priest was arriving. Kumara and Suresha washed the body, quietly thinking about the last time they did this together for Vijay.

The two men struggled to carry the body. Suresha was not very strong and had become quite portly over the last few years. He huffed and puffed through the procession, following the priest to the cremation grounds.

Geetha went to retrieve Anu from the neighbor. The midwife had already been and gone, saying the girl was getting ready to deliver and that the baby would come soon. By the time the men returned from the cremation, Anu had delivered her first son.

"Ah, Kumara, you are back. Come. See what your bride has done for you. Look, a son."

Kumara knelt by Anu's side, trying to get a glimpse of the baby's face, which was pressed into her breast.

"It's a boy," she whispered. He stroked the baby's head, wishing his father had waited just one more day to at least see the baby.

"Don't you have anything to eat here? Go, get some food for her."

Kumara walked out into the early morning darkness. He approached the food vendors on the edge of the main street, wondering how hungry Anu might be after delivering their baby.

CHAPTER 28

It was almost six months before Umesh received a response from Delhi. Apparently, Dr. Gupta had died, and his letter had been shuffled around for some time before someone decided to answer. It was a long letter that lavished praise on Dr. Gupta, and listed all the major milestones of the Drugs Commission since 1930. The work of the Commission had culminated in a second Drugs Act being passed in 1945, but there was a ten-year time period for implementation. The letter outlined several pages of license requirements that would be enforced at some point. These included licenses for any type of drug trade imaginable, even one that covered drugs being sold from the back of a truck or motorcycle. The letter was signed by Dr. Anand.

Umesh laughed at the ambitious litany of rules and regulations and wondered how on earth the government intended to enforce them. In any case, if he understood the requirements, each applicant had to have the express supervision of a pharmacist or a doctor to be granted a license. There weren't enough doctors, let alone pharmacists, in India to cover every single seller of drugs. It was a recipe for patronage, corruption, and bribery. It was a self-dealing act for the bureaucracy, and Umesh was glad he was out of the business.

The letter closed by making an unambiguous request for money before the application forms would be sent. That was on top of the fees that would be required upon submission. Umesh shook his head. Clearly, the culture of money was not the sole province of the movie industry, and here was proof that it was rampant throughout the ranks of the newly independent government.

He started to draft a response, asking for the application papers to be sent to him for a license to cover three shops. The bribe was a different matter. He would have to send someone with the money to Delhi, along with the letter. It would take at least ten days to travel there by train and back. He would have liked to send Geetha, but he knew she could not leave her business for that long. He would speak to Sanjay about it that evening during their time together.

"Sanjay, I need to send someone to Delhi with a letter and money. Who do you think we can send on this errand?"

"Oh, we should send Ravi. I think we sent him a few times to Bangalore with messages for some of your colleagues. He always came back. He is trustworthy."

"Yes, Sanjay, but Delhi is not like Bangalore. He is an old man. I am worried he will get killed for the money or get lost in Delhi."

Sanjay laughed.

"Well, sir, if you want, I can go, but it means I will be gone from here for almost fifteen days."

"You are an old man also. If someone wanted to rob you, I am sure they would hurt you as well, and I can't have that. Anyway, I need you here."

"Well, you can send Vivek, but then you won't have a driver for several days."

"Maybe you can find me a temporary driver. There are many boys who know how to drive now in Mysore. Maybe Lathika's aunt can loan us her driver. She doesn't go out much these days since she got sick."

"Ah, that's a good idea, sir. I will try to arrange it. But perhaps you would mention to Madam that I will ask her aunt this favor."

"Of course. I will do so tonight."

Sanjay told Vivek of his mission that evening.

"Why do I have to go to Delhi? Who will drive the master? What is this errand for?"

"It is for the woman whose nephew you killed. It is a penance for you." Sanjay smiled slyly.

"I'm not going on some stupid errand for that woman. She is a piece of dirt and doesn't deserve anything from me."

"The master has decided. It is done. You will go as soon as I can arrange for Madam's aunt's driver to help us while you are away."

Vivek rolled his eyes and stamped his feet on the way out.

The substitute driver drove him to the Bangalore train station. Sanjay went with them and gave instructions throughout the whole journey.

"First, you must go to Kalyan. This journey is very long, and you will stop in many villages. You may have time to get off the train for a short while, but you must be careful to be alert when it is leaving so you don't get stuck and have to wait for the next one. Do you understand?"

Vivek grimaced and nodded his head.

"I promise I will only get off if I need to relieve myself," he snickered.

"Well that is fine, but just don't go too far. Someone will jump you and steal your money if you are not careful. Make sure you get off at Kalyan. You must not go any further, or you will end up in Mumbai, and this will be a bad thing. Do you understand?"

Vivek was getting tired of the lecture.

"Yes, yes, I understand."

"When you get to Kalyan, you must get a ticket for Allahabad. Can you remember that name?"

"A-lla-ha-bad," he mimicked slowly.

"Are you making fun of me?" Sanjay was now angry with him.

"No, no sir, not me."

"I don't know how far it is from Kalyan to Allahabad. But you can ask one of the guards. Anyway, when you arrive in Allahabad you must get a ticket for Delhi. From there, I don't know how many villages you will pass, but Delhi will be the end of the line, so they will make sure you get off."

By now, Vivek was even more unenthusiastic about this journey. How long was it going to take?

"When you get to Delhi, you will have to find out the location of the Office of the Drugs Commission. When you arrive there, you will give the guard the letter from Mr. Umesh so that he will let you see the Assistant to the President of the Commission, Dr. Anand. You must not give the second letter or the money to anyone except him. Do you understand?"

"Yes, yes, this is obvious."

"Well, I am sure they will try to tell you that you cannot see him and that they will take the message to him for you. You must stand firm. You can tell them that your master promised to kill you if you give the letter to anyone else," Sanjay laughed.

"Even if they beat me?"

"Yes, even if they beat you. And, Mr. Umesh said that you must bring back papers for him from the Commission. It is very important. They will tell you to go away, that they will send the papers in the mail, but you must tell them no, that you will wait for them to prepare the papers so you can bring them back with you."

Sanjay had strapped the letter and the money onto Vivek's skin around his belly. He'd also given him a separate pouch of money for his train fares and food.

"You must be careful. There are many bad people in Delhi. They will try to rob you or even kill you. If you see people fighting and shouting in the streets, stay away. There are a lot of riots and bad things happening in these places."

"Do they kill each other in the streets?"

"Yes, Mr. Umesh has told me that there is a lot of killing of Muslims these days in Delhi. You are a Hindu, so you should be alright. Just don't get caught in the middle of anything."

Vivek knew about Muslims but had never met one. These were people who didn't believe in Hindu gods, and they ate cows.

"Oh, and I forgot to tell you, once you arrive in Kalyan, no one will speak your language. You will have to speak English to everyone."

Vivek was very proud of his English language skills. As Mr. Umesh's driver, it was expected that he would be able to communicate in English and had worked hard to gather his limited vocabulary. But by the time they reached the station, he had lost some of his swagger and was very quiet. It was time to go.

Vivek was used to the crowds on the streets and had been to Bangalore many times. This was the easy part of the journey. He left the safe harbor of the boss's Rolls Royce and plunged into the crowd, looking for the right platform to Kalyan.

Sanjay was silent on the journey back to Mysore. He figured it would take a long time for Vivek to return. And while he was pretty sure that, barring murder, an accident, or illness, his messenger would come back, there was always a chance that he would run. As they drove on, he noticed a brand new moon over the horizon. If he wasn't back by the next new moon, he would start to worry.

Vivek eventually found his platform and boarded. He'd never actually traveled on a train and was quite excited at the prospect. It was not such a long one, maybe four or five carriages, of which only one was reserved for lower castes. It wasn't too crowded when he got there, and he claimed a spot on the floor underneath a window where he could lean against the side of the carriage. He had no idea when they would leave. It was getting dark, and he eventually dozed off. The jolt of the departure ritual with the groan of the wheels and the hissing of steam woke him several hours later. By then, the carriage was full of people, mostly men, but he noticed a few families with children camping in the center.

They traveled through the night, making several stops. Vivek didn't dare leave his carriage at the first two stops, but by the third one, having learned that there was no quick turnaround, he stepped off briefly just to relieve himself and buy some food. At each stop, he would ask the passengers around him if the next one was Kalyan, but most just shrugged. It seemed no one had made this trip before, and he wondered, but didn't ask, why all these people were going to Kalyan. Sanjay had warned him to keep to himself and not get cozy with anyone, either onboard the train or off.

A DANGEROUS TIME

By the second morning, they reached Kalyan, and Vivek felt a bit more confident. Maybe this wasn't such a bad errand after all. He stood up and looked out the window. All he could see were trees, hills, and forests behind the two low-down huts on the side of the tracks. There was no city; there were no markets or temples like you would see in Bangalore. Bewildered, he went looking for the ticket office to get his ticket for the next leg of the journey. This station was in the middle of nowhere. He just hoped Sanjay was right and that this was the right place to get the train to Allahabad.

It was his first opportunity to practice his English.

"Allahabad?" he asked very politely at the ticket counter.

"Two rupees," the ticket clerk said, holding up two fingers.

"When is going?" he asked as he paid his fare.

"I don't know, maybe tonight, maybe tomorrow. You just go to the track." He pointed back toward the platform.

He waited until nightfall for the train, and it was another two days and nights before they arrived in Allahabad. This place was a bit more lively than Kalyan. As he descended, he saw what looked like a small temple alongside the tracks. It had a blue egg-shaped dome and a half-moon symbol at the top. An awning was set up on one side, with blankets spread out on the ground. A group of men wearing skull caps were gathered just behind. Suddenly, he heard loud, mournful singing coming from the building. The men got down on their knees and prostrated themselves. They would then sit back on their heels and repeat the action. They did this several times until the chanting stopped and everyone went on their way.

He didn't know what that was all about, but he was thirsty and hungry and wanted to make sure he got his ticket before attending to his needs.

"Delhi, please?"

"Three rupees."

He knew what three meant. He could count to ten in English. He proudly took three rupees out of his pouch and passed them over. He knew better than to ask what time it would leave. He was a quick study, and it had become clear that one just waits by the side of the tracks until the porters and the crowd start clamoring for the name of the destination city as the train slowly rolled up to the platform.

Vivek stopped at a tea stall for a drink. He pointed to the little blue-domed building and asked the vendor in English:

"What is please?"

"Masjid," was the reply.

"Masjid?" repeated Vivek. "What is masjid?"

"Masjid for Muslims pray."

Vivek didn't know what the English words "masjid" or "pray" meant, but he heard the word "Muslim" loud and clear. He'd forgotten about them after he'd left Bangalore and heard all of Sanjay's horror stories. He carefully sized up the tea vendor. There was no way to tell if the man was a Muslim; he wasn't wearing those skullcaps he saw on the men in the domed temple. He looked around, warily wondering if there were more Muslims there on the platform. He glanced back toward the building where the chanting had come from, wondering if it was a temple for the Muslims to worship in.

He made sure to put some distance between himself and the Muslim temple before he sat down to wait. The platform was very quiet, but as the afternoon wore on, people started to arrive in great numbers, carrying cases, boxes, and sacks. Vivek assumed that this next leg to Delhi would be far more busy than the last, given that they were going to the big city. Sure enough, by the time the train arrived in the early evening, the platform was mobbed with travelers. He would have to fight his way in to get a place to sit.

CHAPTER 29

After traveling through the night, they finally arrived early in the morning. Vivek stepped off and felt something very different. The air was cool, not hot like it always was in Mysore. He shivered as he walked out of the station onto the street. Not far from him, he saw an enormous castle with two square towers capped by large domes and many flags flying from the roof. What amazed him was the color of the stones. They were dark red, and the entire building looked like it had been dipped in the henna that women would use on their arms and faces during weddings. He was drawn to the building, in awe of the size and imposing facade. He stared at it for a long time; it was an overwhelming end to the many hours of waiting and riding the trains. He looked around, dazed by the crowds, the motorcycles, bicycles, automobiles, and tuk-tuks all moving at a speed he was not used to. How would he find the place where he had to take the message from Mr. Umesh?

India Gate. It was the landmark that Sanjay had told him he had to find first. It would be close to the government building for his errand. He looked around, wondering who he could ask for directions. He crossed the busy street toward some stalls that were lined up facing the station. He studied the faces of the shopkeepers, looking for someone with kind features that he could ask. He decided on the oldest-looking man and practiced the words in his head before very politely asking:

"Babu, can you help me? I must go to India Gate."

"Yes, yes, I can help you. You must go from here down this road. Just follow the automobiles until you reach Connaught Place. You will know when you reach it. It is a very big roundabout. From there, you will see the India Gate."

"Thank you, Babu, thank you very much." Vivek heard "Connaught Place" and "roundabout" and hoped these were landmarks on the way to his destination.

He started to walk in the direction that was shown him. The roads in Delhi were very wide, and all the buildings were quite big, but the street shops and people he saw were not so different from Bangalore. He did see, however, a lot of people with lighter skin color, and he also saw many of the skull caps worn by the Muslims he had seen in Allahabad. If he saw any of them approaching from the other direction, he quickly got out of their way, afraid that one of them would jump on him to kill him. But no one paid attention to him, and he finally made it to Connaught Place.

Ha, he thought to himself, this is just like KR Circle. Maybe a bit bigger and grander, but certainly the same idea. He smiled, very pleased with himself. He could see the square outline of what had to be the India Gate off in the distance, in the haze of the now-hot sun. The old man was right. It was obvious what it was.

Vivek hurried on, dodging the automobiles and trams as he crossed the wide and busy streets. The road was completely straight, like a rope he could follow to his destination. When he arrived at the monument, it was not at all clear what to do next. There were no buildings directly around the Gate; it was surrounded by an even bigger roundabout and green parks and gardens. He had to think hard to remember the English name of the place he had to go to. Drugs. Something to do with drugs. Maybe it was the Drugs Office? It was worth a try, but he wasn't entirely sure how to tackle this next phase of his mission. The area he would have to cover was vast, and it was already midday. Best he could expect was that he would find the right building by nightfall, then hope to deliver the letter in the morning. If Delhi government was anything like Bangalore, the officials would all be going home soon.

Vivek decided to go left. He planned to walk around the roundabout and check out the heavy, square buildings laid out on the side streets radiating from the Gate. It was going to take time. The first building he arrived at had two tall guards standing at the door. They were Sikhs. He knew this from their very elaborate turbans and their mustaches and beards. He had seen some of these people in Bangalore, mostly around the British Cantonment area. He eyed them carefully, fully expecting a kick or the butt of a rifle in his chest if he asked them anything. But it had to be done. He drew in a long breath and asked in English:

"Sir, please, my master give me message for Drugs Office. Where is please?"

The two Sikhs looked at each other, then back at Vivek.

"What did you say? I cannot understand you."

This was a problem. Vivek didn't understand. He smiled at the man and repeated, this time, using his arm to indicate, generally, behind him.

The two men spoke to each other, laughing and shaking their heads.

"Where are you coming from?" one asked in English.

This Vivek could understand. They were asking him where he was from. Maybe they hadn't understood his question.

"Yes, sir, I am coming from Mysore," he said proudly. "Where is Drugs Office please?"

Mysore meant nothing to the guards.

"I don't know a Drugs Office. But wait here. I will see if I can find out for you."

Vivek didn't understand, but the men seemed to be friendly. He was lucky. It could have turned out very differently. He had seen such soldiers in Bangalore kick and hit low-caste people just for sitting or squatting on the street.

One of the Sikhs went inside the building, while the other signaled with his hand to Vivek to sit down. He lit a cigarette and offered one to Vivek. He was stunned by this behavior, as he would not have expected such familiarity from a Sikh toward him. In any case, he refused the cigarette, but smiled widely, saying, "Thank you, thank you."

When the other guard returned, the two had a long discussion before turning to him.

"You must go across the India Gate park, to the other side of the roundabout. There you will find a very big group of buildings. That is the High Court of Delhi. Then, you must ask someone for the Drugs Commission Bhavan. If you are lucky, someone will know it and show you the way."

The jumble of words came too fast. He stared back at the man, smiling, trying to piece together what he heard.

He looked back toward the gate, pointing his finger.

"This way? Please?"

The Sikhs laughed again. He laughed along, hoping their good nature would continue.

"Come," said one of the guards and walked Vivek back to the main roundabout.

"You go this way," he said, pointing his finger directly across the square. "You must find the Delhi High Court. Do you understand? Delhi High Court." This time, the guard spoke very slowly.

Vivek repeated, "Delhi High Court."

"Good, then, after this, you must find Drugs Commission Bhavan."

This time Vivek recognized the word "Drug" and thought he understood. He smiled again at the man, repeating:

"Delhi High Court, Drugs Commission Bhavan."

"Yes, yes, you can give your message to the Drugs Commission Bhavan."

The Sikh patted him on the shoulder and left him on the side of the square to head back to his post. Vivek was trying to decide whether to cross the square directly or to walk all around it to the opposite side. If he walked around, he would have to cross five or six roads to get to the other side. It looked to him though, like there was a straight path that cut right through the massive park. His only hesitation was that he had to cross the main road of the roundabout to get to the center span, then cross the road again on the other side of the park, but crossing only two roads seemed better to him than six. He looked at all the vehicles whizzing by, wondering if there would come a lull for him to make a run for it. After waiting some time with no luck, he decided that he would have to cross, and just dodge the traffic as it came.

Vivek started to sprint. Some of the vehicles would slow down when they saw him, but others, like the tuk-tuks, just kept on coming and would have hit him if he didn't jump out of the way. He had to run, stop, jump aside, run again, go back a few steps, and finally, panting and out of breath, he made it across to the center of the square. As he approached, the Gate got bigger and bigger, until standing under it, he couldn't even see the top anymore. Nothing in Mysore or Bangalore could compare to this structure.

By the time he crossed the second span of the roundabout and found his way to the Drugs Commission Bhavan, it was closed. He found some food stalls, but the food didn't look at all familiar or appetizing to him. But he was starving, so he ate a couple of pakoras anyway and settled down on a side street near the Drugs building to wait for morning.

He was very apprehensive for the next day. This was the key to his whole mission in coming to Delhi. Sanjay had told him that he must return home with a packet of papers for Mr. Umesh. He fingered the letter he had to pass on to Dr. Anand, hoping things would go smoothly.

CHAPTER 30

At daylight, Vivek stood up, dusted himself off, and walked toward the grand entrance of the building. His white shirt was by now quite dingy, and his trousers showed the many hours of travel all too well. Since he'd become Mr. Umesh's driver, he was very fastidious about his appearance. Driving an important man required a commensurate amount of attention to his clothing to represent his boss well. He knew he didn't cut a very dashing figure by this time in his trip, so he worried about the impression he would make.

He waited for the guards to show up at the front door. This time, the guards were not Sikhs but rather men dressed in uniforms that looked like police. Vivek practiced the words in his head before approaching the two men.

"Please sir, I have message for Dr. Anand."

The guards sized him up and started to laugh.

"Get away from here, you dog," shouted one, lifting his baton in a threatening way.

Vivek cringed but held his ground. He realized he'd forgotten the second part of his speech.

"Please sir, I have message for Dr. Anand from Mr. Umesh NV Mysore."

"If you don't leave I will kick you and have you taken to jail," was the response, which of course, Vivek did not understand.

He smiled, bowing his head in quick succession, wondering if he got through.

"Please sir, I have message for Dr. Anand from Mr. Umesh NV Mysore."

The guard lunged and cracked him over the head with his baton.

He retreated a few steps, thinking that he might try again a bit later, hoping these two might be in a better mood. He fell back to the corner of the road, where he could see the entrance and the people coming and going. After some time, the two original guards were replaced by two new ones. Vivek was waiting for this opening and went straight up to them.

"Please, sir, I have message for Dr. Anand from Mr. Umesh NV Mysore."

The two started talking to each other, but Vivek couldn't understand. It didn't sound like English. He looked from one guard to the other, smiling.

"Dr. Anand. Who is Dr. Anand?"

Vivek wasn't sure what to say.

"Drugs Commission Bhavan," he remembered what the Sikh had told him. "I have message for Dr. Anand from Mr. Umesh NV Mysore."

Given that these two hadn't yet threatened him with harm, he risked showing them the short English message that Umesh had given him introducing Vivek as his messenger and requesting that Dr. Anand see him. Umesh had carefully worded the letter so the reader would understand that Vivek would only hand over the message to Dr. Anand and not anyone else.

Neither of the guards could read, but they studied the piece of paper carefully. Finally, one of them went inside the building and returned with a very old, very thin man with round spectacles, wearing trousers and a jacket like he had seen Mr. Umesh wear many times.

The old man read the note, looked at Vivek, and spoke to the guards again in a language Vivek knew was not English. Who were these people? he thought. Hopefully, they weren't Muslims, intent on robbing then killing him.

He watched as the man went back into the building. This didn't look good, and he wasn't sure what to do next.

"Please sir, I have message for Dr. Anand from Mr. Umesh NV Mysore."

The guards laughed, and one of them nodded.

"Yes, yes, Dr. Anand is coming."

CHAPTER 31

Finally, Vivek was relieved of the bribe to Dr. Anand and Mr. Umesh's letter, and these were replaced two days later by the precious bundle of papers that he had to bring back. He hid them in his shirt as he tried to retrace his route all the way back to the station, making a few missteps and having to double back a few times. By the time he reached the platform, the train for Allahabad was gone, and he would have to wait until the next day.

He arrived in Bangalore a week later and went to Mr. Umesh's office to wait until his master showed up. He was glad to be on familiar turf again. Back in Mysore, he became a celebrity with all the servants, showing off with stories of all his adventures. Many of them had never been to Bangalore, let alone anywhere as exotic as Delhi. Vivek described the trains and the stations, the Muslims, the people and the different color of their skin, the cold weather, the red fort in Delhi, the grand monuments, and the sheer scale of the roads and roundabouts. He didn't realize he would be making the same trip again a few weeks later, this time to deliver the completed application back to Dr. Anand for the pharmacy license.

If Vivek was a bit cocky before, now that he'd been to Delhi twice, he became even more so. He drove a bit faster, rolled his eyes more, stomped his feet, and complained more confidently whenever he was sent on errands.

"Mr. Umesh, I want to talk to you about Vivek." Sanjay was at his nightly meeting with his boss.

"I think we should send him to Bangalore to see Mrs. Geetha. He should give her the news about the application you sent to Delhi. It will be a good lesson for him to see the woman whose nephew he killed."

Umesh threw his head back and laughed.

"So my driver is getting a bit too big for his boots, eh?"

"Yes sir, yes sir. You have guessed it. I think he needs to be taken down a few pegs," Sanjay smiled.

"Good, yes. Next time he drives me to Bangalore, he can do this. It is an excellent idea. Just make sure he tells her we don't know how long it will take to get the license. Delhi government moves very slowly."

"Yes, I will make sure, Master."

Vivek was, of course, angry about his errand.

"Why do I have to do this? Why can't you go yourself to tell this woman?"

"The master has decided. It is done. You must go to her shop in the station and tell her. You must give the message only to her, do you understand?"

"What if she is not there? What do I do then? You don't want me to be late to pick up Mr. Umesh?"

"Don't worry about that. It is very important that you deliver the message to her. He will wait for you."

He turned and stormed out of the room. Why were they doing this to him?

The next time he drove to Bangalore, he went to find the stall in the train station. It had a big red cross painted outside.

"I am here to see Mrs. Geetha."

"She is not here. Can I help you? What is it you want to buy?"

"When will she return?"

"Mrs. Geetha is hardly coming to this shop. She is a very busy lady. What do you want? Why are you looking for her?"

Vivek hesitated. He knew he'd been told to wait for her and under no circumstances to give the message to anyone but her. But if she never came there, what was he to do? He didn't want to be confronted by that woman again. He wondered if he could get away with it.

"I have a very important message for her from Mr. Umesh. I am his driver," he said, puffing up his chest.

Kumara stared at him for a long time before answering. So this was the man who had killed Vijay. He measured his words out very slowly.

"I know who you are. You killed my brother."

Stunned, Vivek's eyes flashed from side to side as he tried to avoid looking straight at Kumara. All he could think of was that Sanjay had set him up, and that this had been his plan all along. He tried several times to say something, but the words wouldn't come out of his mouth. His hands were sweating, and he rubbed them together so hard that his fingers turned red. He wanted to turn and run, but his knees were shaking, and he thought if he moved, he might collapse to the ground.

"You'd better give me the message for Mrs. Geetha," Kumara finally said.

"I went all the way to Delhi two times for your license," he finally blurted out.

"Well then, where is it?"

"Mr. Umesh said it may take some time. They will send it to him in the post. Then I will bring it to you."

"Now go, get out of my sight." Kumara flipped his hand at Vivek.

He wasn't sure he'd heard correctly. Was he being dismissed? He couldn't believe it. But Kumara's open hand pointing towards the exit was clear. He found the will to turn and run out of the shop before anything else was said.

Kumara looked after him, suddenly angry at himself that he hadn't berated and shouted at the driver. It was too late now. But he wasn't really sure what he should have said. It wasn't clear to him that Vivek felt any remorse at all. He shook his head. It had been a long time since Vijay's death, but seeing that man had brought all the sadness back into his mind. He held back his tears as he turned to serve his next customer. I hope I never see that man again, he thought.

PART VII
MIGRATION

CHAPTER 32

He woke up choking. It took him a few seconds to grasp what was happening. At first, he thought it was his wife lighting up her opium pipe, but quickly, he felt the sting in his eyes from the black smoke filling the room. He tried to shake her awake. His son and daughter had already opened their eyes.

"Come, come, it is a fire. We have to go now!"

The flames had come through the adjacent dwelling into their room. He tried to lift his drowsy and still-stoned wife by the shoulders. His son came to help him, but he pushed him away.

"Go, go, get your sister and get out. I will come behind you!"

The young man grabbed his disoriented sister by the wrist and dragged her toward the opening of the room, which he could not see through the smoke. Once outside, they had to move a long way off to escape the flames and smoke billowing from the row of huts. People were running and screaming from the inferno. He glanced behind him, expecting to see his father and mother emerge from the chaos. Many of his neighbors were around him, but he did not see his parents. He pushed his sister to the ground and ran back toward their room.

He jumped through a gap in the flames, not knowing what was on the other side. He stumbled over something and, without being able to see, felt around it to make out what it might be. It was a body. Without going further, he heaved it over his shoulder and ran back. His feet and arms were smoldering, and his shirt was burning on his back. He couldn't see where he had left his sister, but as soon as he cleared the flames, he lay the body down. It was his mother. He turned back, trying to figure out how to dodge the flames to get back to his father. He started to sprint toward the fire, but now several of his neighbors held him back.

"You can't go back in there. You will die. There is no one left alive in there!"

He shrugged out of their grasp and ran back toward their room. But there was no gap in the fire this time. He grabbed hold of his head and started to wail. He beat his head with his fists, then squatted on the ground, watching the fire burn. His face was black with soot, and the sting on his flesh was starting to ache. Soon, he would be in agony from the burns.

He stayed for a long time, watching until the fire burned itself out. Finally, accepting that his father was not going to walk out, he stood and turned away from the ashes.

He found his sister with their mother's head in her lap. He wondered if she was alive. Kneeling down, he took her hand. Peering into her face, he tried to see if she was breathing.

"Go find some water," he told his sister. She stood up, looking around, bewildered by the scene around her. There was nothing, not a container, not a cup, nothing that she could use to bring water. She started to run toward the village well, hoping that she might find something or someone who would help.

"Ah, my son, it is you!" His mother opened her eyes. "What is this? What have you been doing? Your face is all black!"

"There has been a fire, Amma. We have lost everything. Father is dead."

"What? Father is dead? How can that be?"

She was still disoriented from her opium-induced sleep. He had seen it many times since her last child, his brother, had died a few years ago. She had been in so much pain after the delivery; there had been so much blood that none of them thought she would live. Instead, the baby died, and she survived, aided by the opium that was now a constant in their lives. He knew that soon she would be looking for a hit to soothe her anxiety.

"How could you let this happen?" she wailed at him. "What are we going to do? How will we live?"

"It is the same for everyone in our village. They came in the night and set fire to the homes."

"Who did this? Who would do such a thing?"

"People are saying it was the muhajir coming into our village for land."

"I don't understand...your father said they would never come so far up the valley. He said they were all going to Karachi, and that no one would come here." She was shouting at him. "Where is your father?"

"I told you, he is gone. He was burned in the fire."

He stood up, looking around for his sister. There were groups of his neighbors, all huddled, sitting on the ground. He glanced back to where the row of huts used to be, wondering if there might be anything salvageable. He rummaged around the dying plumes of smoke, kicking over piles of rubble, looking for any sign of his father's body. He saw a lot of black chunks that looked like the coal or cow pats they might burn in their chulha, but he had no way of knowing these were charred bones from those who had perished in the fire.

Walking back to his mother, he saw that his sister had returned with a small tin of water.

"Where is my opium? It was under my shawl when I went to sleep. Go, go find it for me!"

His sister looked up at him with tears in her eyes. Her face was black with soot, her hair matted with flecks of ash. He pulled her aside.

"We have to find some opium for her, or she will go crazy. You stay with her. I will go see if I can get some."

"But everyone has lost everything in the fire."

"I will try it. If not, I will go to the drugs stall tomorrow and see if they will give me some. I will promise to pay them later."

He wandered around the makeshift camp, looking at the weary and hopeless faces of his neighbors. He cringed to ask for money, seeing the destitute situation they were all in. He decided to find the man who ran the drugs stall in the village.

As he walked through, looking for the shopkeeper, he ran into many of his young friends. They were angry, talking of revenge and violence against their attackers.

"We must show these people a lesson," one of them said.

"But who are they? Do we even know how to find them?"

"Yes, they have a camp some distance from here. I know it was them. My brother said they all came across the new border a few months ago. Now they want our land and the fields we work in."

"But what are we supposed to do now? If we rebuild our homes, they will just come again, no?"

"They are saying we have to go south, across the new border. They want us gone from here. This is now a Muslim land."

"We are going to get them in the night. We can get some weapons, knives, and clubs and go into their camp. We have to get even with the deaths they have caused."

"My father is dead," he said quietly.

"And my two small brothers also."

"My mother was burned alive."

The mob came to a consensus to make a raid in the coming days. He moved on, continuing on his mission for his mother. He couldn't find the shopkeeper and decided to go to the stall where he kept his medicines. It had clearly been looted before being torched. He looked around, hoping he could find something that would help her when the wife of the shopkeeper stood up from a small group of people squatting near the shop.

"Ha, are you here looking for my husband? He is dead. We have nothing left!" she wailed.

"Auntie, I need some opium for my mother. My father was burned in the fire, and she is going crazy with grief. I will pay you later, I promise!"

"I have a small bundle that my husband buried behind the stall. I can give you a little, but I only have the nuggets. She will have to eat them."

"Ah, that is so kind and generous of you. I will pay you, I promise…"

"Try to give her a smaller quantity so you can have some for tomorrow. But I see you have many burns on you also?"

"Yes, I went into the fire to save my parents, but I only got to her."

"You must be in pain. You must put some turmeric paste on those as soon as you can. Otherwise, you will be taking the opium yourself!"

The next morning, some of the Hindus from the surrounding villages who had not yet been attacked came to the camp to help. They brought food, water, and clothing for the destitute. But the young men were planning the counterattack into the Muslim camp despite being advised to start moving their families to the other side of the border.

He joined in the raid. He wasn't sure he could hurt another person, but by the time they reached the camp in the dead of night, the whole group was whipped up into a frenzy. That night, he slashed and clubbed a small boy and two women. He couldn't tell if he had killed any of them as they retreated very quickly to avoid being chased. He was agitated, but also experienced a euphoria he had never felt before.

There was no work, and he had resorted to stealing in the neighboring villages to get food for his sister and drugs for his mother. He knew they couldn't stay.

"Amma, we have to think about heading south."

His mother was only partly lucid.

"You are wrong. We will stay here, where your father has died. I won't go anywhere without him."

"No, you are wrong. They don't want us here. If we stay, we will be killed just like Father."

"But I don't know where to go! We have no one!"

"Don't worry. We will go to Karachi. I heard they are giving Hindus passage on boats to Mumbai. We can live there."

"Mumbai? What is Mumbai? We have no family there!"

"We don't need relatives. We have each other. It is settled."

CHAPTER 33

The now-homeless of his village were joining caravans of other Hindus following the river south to Hyderabad. He tried to get his family onto trucks, but there was always a bribe to pay, and he had no money. Many of the drivers looked lasciviously at his sister, telling him they would take them all the way to Karachi in exchange for a few minutes with her. His mother had already told him to sell her for money for her opium, but he had shouted at her that he would never do that. His entire being was devoted daily to getting opium, getting food, and protecting his sister. The euphoria he felt that day after avenging his father had receded far into the background. He was constantly on edge, begging, stealing, fighting, and crawling a few miles each day toward the coast.

They were sitting at the side of the road to rest for the night. The people around him seemed to think they would arrive in Hyderabad in the next day or so. The rumor was that from there they would be given free rail passage to Karachi.

"Why do you think anyone will just give us a ticket?" his mother asked.

"I am sure there is nothing free. But they want us to leave."

"My son, you'd better go find me some opium for the journey. I don't have much left, you know. I was in agony the other day when you didn't get me enough."

"You are a greedy woman. You know I have become a thief for you."

"Well, I told you what to do. Your sister is worth money. But you won't do as I say. Then it is your fault you are a thief."

He shook his head. Standing up, he walked out on his nightly errand.

Hyderabad was a big, busy, and bustling city compared to the village they had left. If it hadn't been for the collective radar of the refugees, he would have had no idea where to go. Everyone was following someone else blindly, hoping that there was some end to the journey. Eventually, they arrived at an open field where some local Hindus had brought food and water for the tired and dusty crowd.

"What is this place? What will happen to us now?" his sister whispered to him.

"I think we have arrived in Hyderabad. I need to go find out how we can get to Karachi. Stay here with her and cover your head and arms so no one can tell your age."

His mother had taken her dose of opium as soon as they sat down. She would be out for several hours.

A group had gathered around a tent at the far end of the field. He wandered over to see what he could find out.

They were congregated around two old men.

"They have been sent by the Muslims to help us get to Karachi," someone told him.

"How are we going to travel, by truck or train?"

"They didn't say. They are telling us to stay here until they work it out."

"How long will that take? We have already been on the road for many weeks."

"Let's say that the Muslims want us gone, so they will have to figure something out."

"Well, I hope they get us transportation before someone comes and kills us all. We are sitting ducks in this camp."

"You are right, but at least they have organized the local Hindus to bring us food and water. If they wanted to kill us, they would have done so by now, huh?"

He couldn't argue with that logic but was very wary of the situation. He moved on, finding his way into the city to get the next dose of opium for his mother.

"Where is the drugs bazaar here?" he asked the first passerby.

"There is one on the other side of this area. You will see if you go that way, the river splits into two arms. One is going left, the other right. If you follow the left branch, you will find it."

It was a jumble of roads and back streets. The slums he found were far more cramped and overcrowded than anything he had seen on the way from his village. Finally, he stumbled into the market and found his way to the medical shops.

"Grandfather, I need to buy some opium for my father. How much do you want for a small bag?" It was easier to lie. It could raise too many questions if they thought he was buying for a woman.

"I can sell you a bag for two rupees."

"Ah, can you show me the size of this bag please?"

The man lifted a small cloth bag from behind the counter.

"But sir, I am very poor. My father is desperate. Can you make a price for me?"

"Who are you? I have never seen you before in my shop. Why should I make any discount for you? Go on, get out. You can try your con in another shop. Not here!" The man was shooing him out of the stall.

After visiting three stalls, he managed to get a price of one and a half rupees. But first, he had to find the money.

He moved into the main bazaar. There were many people about, and he noticed several small beggar children running around. They were sure to have some money on them. He followed a child who looked like he was three or four years old. He came up to him from behind and pushed him forward. No one paid any attention. The boy went sprawling to the ground, his loot scattering around him. Without stopping, he moved quickly to grab a handful of the coins and disappeared into the crowd.

When he thought he had put a good distance between him and the boy, he stopped to see what he had got. Five rupees. Not bad. If only he had one leg or was deformed he too could do as well.

He arrived back at the camp just in time. The young hoodlums in the camp would be making the rounds, looking for trouble with the women. He found his sister sitting up, holding her stoned mother's hand. She smiled at him.

"Ah, come, see, they brought us some food. You must be very hungry."

She had saved a handful of rice for him in her shawl. He didn't tell her about his night, nor did she ask. By now she was very tired, as she wouldn't sleep while he was away. It was too risky. She lay her head on his thigh, feeling safe. She was asleep almost immediately. He covered her head with her shawl so no one could see how young she was.

The next day, the rumor was swirling that carts were coming to take them to the train station.

"But where will we go on the train?" His sister was nervous.

"Karachi. From there, they are saying we will take a boat to Mumbai."

"A boat?"

"Yes, it will take us over the water to the city."

"You mean, like across the river?"

"No, no," he laughed. "Across the sea. It is much bigger than a river. You will see."

She was bewildered; this undertaking was so frightening to her, after spending her entire short life in a small farming village by the river.

Within a few days, wagons drawn by oxen arrived to take them to the train. There was such a clamor to get on them. It was all he could do to keep the three of them together. Everyone was pushing and yelling. All the commotion had the children scared, and there was a lot of wailing and crying.

"Come," he said, dragging his sister by the wrist and pushing his mother. "You must stay in front of me!"

His mother was at least compliant, but his sister kept being dragged back by all the people shoving their way in front of her. He lifted his mother from behind while others on the cart pulled her from her arms. He looked back into the tidal wave of people, trying to find his sister, hoping they could all get on the same cart. Luckily, the crowd was pushing her along until, eventually, he was able to grab her and hoist her onto the wagon.

As the three of them huddled together. His sister looked at him and smiled.

"What is so funny?"

She didn't answer, but instead grabbed his hand, squeezing hard. He smiled back at her, their shared triumph bringing them a moment of relief. After all the walking, waiting, and confusion, it finally felt like something was happening.

CHAPTER 34

The journey on the carts was quick. By nightfall, they were all sitting on the platform, waiting for a train to take them somewhere else. But when it arrived and everyone stood up to fight their way on board, several men descended and blocked entry to the crowd. They started to lead the women into certain carriages and barred the men from entering, pushing and pointing them to carriages further down the line. When he realized what was happening, he took his sister's hand.

"Look, they are Muslims. They are separating the men from the women. You must take Mother and stay close to the door of the carriage so you can get off quickly. I will find you."

He held back, watching and waiting to see which carriage they would get on. He hurried to the closest adjacent one onto which they were herding the men. He was very fearful during the day-long journey. He hoped they were headed for Karachi. The train kept stopping ominously, and he craned to look out of the windows, half expecting a mob to attack. He had heard of such stories from some of the people they were traveling with.

"Do you know where we are going?" he asked an old man sitting next to him.

"Karachi."

"Are you sure? I heard of this, but nothing is certain."

"Yes, you are right. Nothing is certain. This is what I was told. We shall see if we arrive there alive, all of us."

They finally reached their destination and the doors opened. Relieved that the journey was over, he pushed his way out, hurrying to find his mother and sister. He fell onto the platform, looking across to the carriage he had seen them enter. He ran up and down the tracks, searching in the chaos of people. They weren't there.

He thought it might be best to wait until the crowds on the platforms thinned out. But what if they had been murdered or taken by someone? These thoughts had filled his mind during the journey. All he could do was search for them.

As he walked up and down the platform, he noticed the arcade underneath the station arches. He stepped inside, looking left and right when he noticed his sister's dirty shawl that was green at the start of their journey.

"You are safe." This was all he could blurt out as he embraced her tightly.

"Yes, I did as you said. We stayed by the door and were able to get out without being trampled. But she is already asking for her opium."

"She can wait. I have some in my pocket that I didn't give her," he whispered in her ear.

"Ah my son, you have found us! Come, you have to find some opium for me. I was afraid you might have run away and left us!"

"Mother, we can't stop for the opium now. We have to find our way down to the boats so we can get out of Karachi."

"What do you mean? Why do you say this? Why can't we stay here?"

"I have told you this so many times now. The Muslims don't want us here. If we stay, we will be murdered. In fact, I am amazed that we made it so far safely."

His mother stared at him, trying to process this information as if it was the first time she had really heard it.

"Come," he said. "We have to find the Hindus we traveled with so we can follow them to the boats." He looked around, afraid that the convoy had long gone. They would have to find their way alone, without the cover of the sanctioned group.

He would have to ask for directions from someone. This was very dangerous, as the likelihood of revealing they were Hindus would be great. He looked around, studying the clothes and faces of the people on the platform, trying to assess his best chances.

Finally, he settled on one of the porters. He was older, and even though he was wearing a Muslim skull cap, he decided to approach.

"Old Father, can you please tell me how to get to the place where the boats are going from? I am traveling with my old mother who is sick, and my sister. Please, can you help us?"

"You must walk down this road until you see the large circular building with a dome. From there, you will see the water and a bridge. You must cross the bridge by foot until you see the area where the boats are leaving from."

"Good Father, thank you for this. We have been traveling a long time, and my family is hungry. Might you have a few coins for me so I can buy them something to eat?" He knew the man was poor, but since he was being friendly, he thought he'd press his luck.

The man sighed, looking around to see if anyone was paying attention to them. He dug into his pocket and brought out a few rupees.

"Here, this is all I have. You will have to make do. Now go, hurry before someone realizes who you are."

It was clear to the old man who these people were. He knew that the Hindus were being rounded up and moved out because of the partition. He had heard of all the massacres and killings and was ambivalent to help them. But he had many Hindu friends who had already left. He remembered their frightened faces, their bundles, the old, the children, and the fathers and sons trying to protect their families.

CHAPTER 35

The circular building was immense.
"This one is even bigger than the train station!" his sister whispered.

"Come, don't gawk. We need to hurry across the bridge and see if we can find the others."

He dragged his mother along, worried that the boat would have already left. The bridge was lined with food vendors and carts with everything you could imagine for sale.

"Ha, stop, stop. I want to eat something. Maybe one of these vendors has opium!" She was leaning back, trying to break her son's fast stride.

"We can't stop now. We have to go find out about the boat. Then I will get you some food."

He gestured to his sister to grab his mother's other arm, and the two of them moved the old woman quickly across the bridge. He thought he could see a crowd of people milling around in the distance. Maybe, he thought, maybe we will be lucky and in time.

In fact, when they arrived at the dock, he recognized many of the faces. These were the Hindus who had been traveling with them for the last several weeks. But many more had joined the caravan, perhaps three times the number they had started with.

"Stay here while I go and see what is happening."

He moved towards the edge of the dock. Looking around, he tried to find someone who either looked official or not as frightened as everyone else. There was no boat waiting at the pier. He saw two men sitting on a big coil of thick, slimy ropes, smoking cigarettes.

"Is this the place where the Hindus are being given passage to India?"

"I think so, but no one is telling us anything. You can wait here with the others. Someone will come."

"Is there a boat going from here to India?"

"Yes, yes, it is going to Mumbai."

"When will it arrive?"

"Maybe today, maybe tomorrow."

He didn't think he would get any more information from these two, so he kept on walking down the dock. He stopped at one of the family groups sitting down.

"Have you come here to get the boat to India?" he asked the oldest member of the group.

"Yes, we arrived here yesterday. They told us on the way that we could take the boat to Mumbai from here."

"Did they say when this would happen?"

"Maybe tomorrow, maybe the next day, who knows. We are just grateful we haven't lost anyone on the way."

He walked on, wondering if he had enough time to find a bazaar where he could get some more opium for the journey. He had no idea how long the boat would take, and he didn't want to deal with his mother getting frantic and hallucinating on the trip.

Reluctantly, he walked back to the two dock hands.

"Is there a drugs bazaar somewhere here? I need to get some medicine for my mother. She is sick."

"If you go back across the bridge, go down to the water. There you will see a big market with everything you want."

The old man at the train station had given him a couple of rupees, but he needed more money to get enough opium for a few days. Not familiar with his surroundings, he would have to resort to one of his usual crimes to get what he needed. But he would wait until nightfall.

"You must wait here with Amma. I will go get some food and some opium for her," he told his sister.

"Wait, my son, don't go. I need something now. I am in such pain from all this walking and running. Can't you give me something?"

"I don't have anything to give you."

"Then take your sister and walk around with her. Someone will give you money for a few minutes with her. I am sure of it!"

He shook his head, looking at his sister. Without answering, he stood up and headed back toward the bridge.

The bazaar was full of people. He circled the area a couple of times, casing the stalls, the cart vendors, and the back alleys, looking for an opportunity. But first, he had to understand the prices at the drugs bazaar.

He found two young men who had their bicycles parked at the entrance to an alleyway. They had bags and boxes of medicines and pills strapped on their bikes. He wondered if he could grab and run without paying just as one of them handed him the drugs. But there were too many people about.

"How much for your opium?"

"Opium. I don't have any here. But I can get it for you. How much do you need?"

"I need three bags."

"Ten rupees for three bags."

"That is theft. I will only pay you four."

"No, no, this is very hard to find for you. I need at least eight."

"You are crazy. I bought a bag the other day. It was only one rupee," he lied.

The vendor looked at him blankly.

"Forget it. I will go where I won't get robbed."

He turned and walked down the alley, away from the bazaar.

He wandered around the quiet back roads, looking for an opportunity to steal something. Eventually, he came across an old man lying on the ground. He passed him slowly, noticing the stumps of his legs on top of the dirty rags he was sleeping on. The only thing of value he could see was a dirty blanket with red and white stripes wrapped around his head and shoulders. He could easily sell it for three or four rupees. The beggar looked like he was in a drug or alcohol sleep. Looking around to make sure no one was watching, he grabbed the loose end of the shawl from the man's chest and yanked it around and over his head. The back end of the cloth was weighed down by the man's shoulder, but he gave it a good pull, and out it came. The old man never flinched. Maybe he is already dead, he smiled to himself.

He hurried along, folding the blanket into a bundle. Fingering the woolen cloth, he half wondered if he should give it to his sister; it was so soft. He pushed the idea out of his head. There was no time for sentimentality. There were

A DANGEROUS TIME

too many unknowns ahead. He moved back into the bazaar to hawk the blanket off. He would try for ten rupees, hoping to get at least four.

By the time he got back to the dock, his mother was shaking and sweating. His sister was wiping her brow, trying to keep her from flailing her arms about. He pushed one of the nuggets he had bought into her mouth. They both waited for the drug to take effect before saying anything.

"Do you think the boat will come tomorrow?"

"I don't know. I am hopeful it will."

"Will we need money?"

"Everyone here is saying that they are giving Hindus free passage to Mumbai. But just in case, I have a few rupees. Don't let her know though!" He looked down at the now sedated and sleeping old woman. "Listen, I want to tell you something. You must be very careful on the boat. There will be many people very close together. You must keep yourself covered so no one can see your face and arms."

She lifted her soiled shawl and wrapped it around her head, covering her mouth.

"You mean like this?"

He laughed. "Yes, just like that."

CHAPTER 36

They waited two more days before the boat finally arrived. It was nothing like the wooden boats he had seen on the river. It was very tall, maybe four or five levels, and belched steam and black smoke from a chimney in the middle. When it docked, several men wearing funny white garments that stopped above their knees descended from the boat. They were in charge, standing in groups of two and three, talking to each other in a language he couldn't understand. Their skin was milky pale white.

"These are the British..." he whispered to his sister. She couldn't take her eyes off the sailors.

The crowd had risen to their feet in anticipation of boarding. But the white men would not let them onto the boat. He looked around, wondering what the cause of the delay was. Eventually, a lorry arrived, letting out several Muslim guards with long rifles. It wasn't clear what would happen next. He looked at his sister, making sure her face was covered.

The guards circled the refugees, pointing them in the direction of the long ramp onto the ship. The ramp looked very steep, and he was nervous about getting his mother up onto it. The group moved toward the boat, but only one or two persons could fit on the ramp at a time. The logjam slowed the traffic down to a single file. He watched as the two guards on either side of the entrance eyed the travelers, looking for signs of wealth, jewelry, or bundles that they could confiscate and steal. It would be best to have his sister between him and his mother to minimize her exposure to these men.

"Come," he said to her. "You are going to squeeze next to me and help push Mother from behind up that ramp." He didn't want to frighten her. "Just keep your face covered."

Just as he had feared, as they got closer to the gateway, he noticed that several young women, some of them with babies in their arms, had been pulled out of the line and pushed to the side of the boat. He had been told of these abductions by some of his fellow travelers who had had their sisters and, in some cases, their wives taken by the Muslims. He pulled his sister close to his side, keeping her tight between him and his mother.

They had no bags or packages to raise the curiosity of the guards. One look at his toothless mother, with her gray hair disheveled, her eyes half closed, and they moved them along, not paying any attention to the slight figure tucked in between them. She pushed her mother up the ramp while her brother dragged her along, his arm under her shoulders.

The guards had congregated the Hindu group onto the open back deck of the ship. They found a spot to sit down, surrounded by the other refugees. He looked around, sizing up the passengers around them. There was an old man with two small children next to them. Behind were two middle-aged women with a young man, and just in front was a family with three small children. He looked at the wife, wondering how she had made it onto the boat without being pulled aside. They must have paid a bribe, he thought. That was the only explanation.

They waited a long time before the steamship belched its black smoke from the chimney, signaling that they were finally going to move. The gray cloud fell over the decks, with no wind yet to push it away. His sister rubbed her eyes. He noticed how dirty and sooty her face was with all the traveling. Good, he thought. She doesn't look very attractive. We made it this far without her being raped, he thought, and hoped they could finish this journey the same way.

He stood up, feeling confident enough that he might go in search of some food. His mother was calm, and no one seemed to be paying any attention to them.

He was fascinated with the ship. The noise from the engine was deafening, but the breeze he felt as the boat moved forward was refreshing. He leaned over the side rail, watching the sea boil by. For the first time since they had left their burnt-out village, he felt exhilarated, hopeful even. He walked the length of the boat, taking in all the equipment, machinery, ropes, and strange levers and funnels. He had no idea how this thing managed to stay afloat. As he moved towards the front, he found a balcony that looked down onto the lower decks. There, he saw a room with bars across the opening, like a prison. Craning his neck, he tried to see what was inside. Maybe it was tigers, he thought to himself. What he saw though, alarmed him. It was a group of young women, obviously wealthy; he could tell from their clean clothes and colorful shawls. He found his way below to the deck and asked one of the men sitting on the floor who these people were.

"They are the virgins."

"Virgins?"

"Yes. If you have enough money, you can put your sisters there so they will be safe from all the men on this boat."

"Really?"

"Well, there they are, aren't they?"

"Why? Aren't they safe from the men?"

"You never know. It's so crowded on this boat, anything could happen."

Now he wondered whether he had done the right thing, leaving his sister and mother alone on the back deck. The people around them looked benign, he thought, and he hadn't found any food yet.

"Do you know if there are some food vendors on the boat?"

"I think there are some, but you have to go further down in the boat." He pointed to a narrow stairwell around the back of the virgins' cage.

He would have to beg for food. He was nervous to steal on this ship in case he was chased. It wouldn't be easy to slip away. One of the vendors took pity on him and gave him a few spoonfuls of rice wrapped in paper.

He dawdled going back. He was still excited to be on the ship. By now, it was night, and he gazed up at the sky. It was full of stars. It reminded him of the sky at night in his village. He kicked himself for being idle and hurried back to find his family. His mother would be needing her next dose.

CHAPTER 37

He made his way back, craning his neck to see the heads of the two women. As he approached, he could only see his mother. His sister must have finally decided to get some sleep. She would be lying down at her mother's side. As he got closer though, he couldn't see her figure on the deck. His mother was very agitated, looking about, wringing her hands, and hitting herself on the head.

"Ah my son, finally you are here. Go, you must go find your sister. I sent her with this young man behind me to get some money for her. I told him I would split the money with him." She was sobbing, grabbing onto his dirty shirt and trouser legs.

He looked around. The young man and the women who had been behind them were gone.

"Mother, what have you done?" He brought his fists up to his head, preparing to beat her.

"My son, you were gone so long, I thought you had left us. I needed to get some more medicine. It's the only thing I could do! You were gone so long…"

He threw his fists down, turned, and ran back toward the front of the boat, wondering if he could even find her. He looked for her dirty green shawl as he moved through the passengers sitting on the decks. It was nowhere. He wondered if maybe she had been taken somewhere, to a dark corner of the ship for the men to be with her. His pulse quickened and he moved faster. By now, he knew that this boat was like a floating village. You could find everything.

"Hey, someone has taken my sister." He approached one of the food vendors on the lower decks.

He smirked. "You should have locked her up in the virgin cage!"

"I don't have any money. Do you know where they would have taken her?"

"Maybe to the very bottom of the boat, or maybe to where the lifeboats are. Sometimes people use them as a meeting point."

First, he made his way down to the bowels of the ship. He found the place the man told him about. It was right next to where the coal was pushed into the engine of the boat. It was very hot, and the sound from the furnace was deafening. There were blankets laid out on the ground, with men sitting, waiting for their turn with the women behind a dirty cloth that hung like a curtain over some of the pipes and rods. He ran up to it and pulled it aside. He was immediately jumped by two of the pimps who pinned his arms around his back. Before they dragged him out, he got a good look at the three women behind the screen. She wasn't there.

"What, you want to have all three of them?" One of the pimps laughed as he threw him to the ground.

"Someone took my sister," he spat at the man.

"Well, she is not here. These are all my women from Karachi. Now go, get out of here before I kick you."

He scrambled up and ran back to the top deck, falling and tripping, his anger buckling his legs. He made his way back to the front of the ship, where he remembered he had seen the two lifeboats. First, he looked inside them. Nothing. Just as he lifted his head up, he spied two large coils of thick rope behind the boats. In the well of one, he saw her bare legs splayed. Running up to her, he cradled her head and pushed her hair back from her face. She was unconscious. Was she dead? He looked down at her soiled and bloody skirt which was hiked up around her waist. There was a lot of blood. He tried to wake her, but there was no response. He put his ear down to her mouth, listening for her breath. She must be alive, he thought.

He lifted her bony body and carried her back towards their place on the back deck.

"Ah, my son, you found her! Good, good. Did you find the man with my money?"

He didn't answer. He lay his sister down and tried to cover her with his mother's shawl which he grabbed from her shoulders.

Tears welled up in his eyes. He looked around, hoping to see someone who might give him some water. No one lifted a finger to help him. The despair in everyone's eyes around him told him that he was on his own. He lifted her head onto his lap, held her cold hand, and rubbed it between his fingers. At one point, she started to shiver, and he tried to wake her, but she would not respond to his voice or caresses. By the morning, she was dead.

"Look what you have done," his mother screamed at him. "You have killed her! Our only hope for our family, and you have killed her!"

He turned and raised his hand to slap her. She cowered back from him.

"Why do you do this? What have I done? You are an ungrateful son!"

"Mother, you killed her, you fool!"

She started wailing and shouting. "Where is my money? I need some medicine. Someone, please, someone, take pity on an old woman!"

He sat back, watching her carry on for a long time. He pushed a small nugget of opium into her mouth. When she'd quietened down, he went to find one of the deckhands who had helped him before.

"My sister has died in the night. We want to pray and have a ceremony for her."

"Are you crazy? There is no such thing on this ship."

"What am I supposed to do?

"If you have money, you can pay a porter to carry her to the cremation site when we get to Mumbai. You can't leave her here."

"But where can I take her? I don't know anything about this city."

"Well, maybe you can find out this information once you get off the boat. I can't help you."

He fell back in a daze. For a moment, he didn't know where he was. He looked around, wondering how he had come to this place. But the clamoring of the crowd brought him back. They were within sight of Mumbai, and the ship had come alive with anticipation and preparation of the arrival.

PART VIII
PHARMACY LICENSE

CHAPTER 38

The port of Mumbai was immense compared to Karachi. It took the boat half a day to make its way through the bay and the many docks until it finally stopped to let them off. He gathered up his sister's body. He would carry her off the boat to have a cremation ritual for her, but had no idea how to do this in a city he knew nothing about.

As the crowds pushed their way to disembark, he gave his mother another nugget of opium so she would be manageable and calm. He felt a tap on his shoulder and turned. It was an old man from one of the families they had met up with in Karachi.

"My son, I see you are carrying your sister?"

"She died on the ship. I am taking her with me so we can find the cremation grounds."

"The poor child. I will help you. When we get off the ship, your mother can wait with my family. You and I will go find the priest and have the cremation."

The young man was suspicious of the help being offered. He looked at the old man, eyeing his family behind him. There was an older woman, a younger one, and four children of various ages. From the clothing they wore to all the bundles they carried, it seemed to him they were more prosperous than him. He thought it shouldn't be risky to accept their assistance.

"Are you staying here in Mumbai?" he asked.

"No, no. We have relatives in the South. We are headed for Bangalore: my wife, her sister, and her children. Her husband died in the troubles in Karachi."

The young man remembered his own father perishing in the fires, but he did not share any of this history. "Is it very far?" he asked.

"Honestly, I don't know. We will try to get some information from the port on this. But first I will help you with your sister. She should have the proper prayers and cremation."

"I have no money to pay for this. I don't know what to do."

"Don't worry, we are in India now. We will find a way. I will help you."

The refugees were sitting all over the docks. There were many more than had descended from their ship. Perhaps some boats had preceded theirs, all coming from Pakistan to India. He wondered what to do. This was a foreign city to him. They knew no one. Since the old man and his family had been so friendly and welcoming, he wondered if he and his mother should tag along with them to Bangalore. He had no idea where this was and whether he and his mother could make a life there. But if this grandfather was so willing to help him cremate his sister, perhaps he would be willing to let them join his caravan south. It was worth a try, but he would wait until after the death ritual.

He left his mother with the family, secretly giving her another hit of opium to get her through until his return from the cremation. She knew enough to behave in front of strangers. If they knew she was an addict, they might not be so willing to help them.

The two men were gone for a whole day. It took some time to find a priest willing to perform the ritual. He took them to a municipal cremation ground not far from the docks. The rituals were abbreviated, but at least she had a proper cremation. The old man even paid for the priest. He saw him take a bag of money from inside his tunic. He wondered how many more bags he might have hidden with his family's belongings.

"Have you ever been to Bangalore before?"

"Never. My niece is married to a man from there. She has lived there for many years. It is the only family we have in India. Her mother, my sister, died a few years ago. I am hopeful her daughter is still living there and will welcome us."

It seemed like a long shot to him. They were going there with this big family on a prayer. But it was clear the old man had taken a liking to him. Why else would he shell out cash for his sister? Maybe he would even pay for their passage.

"Father, do you think my mother and I can come with you to Bangalore? I have no money, but you have been so kind to us. I can work, I can carry your belongings if you wish. I can help you."

"Yes, my son. I was going to ask you myself if you would come with us. I am an old man; looking after the women and the children is not easy for me. You can help me."

He stared at the old man. I couldn't even take care of my sister, he thought, and this one wants me to guard his family. Tears welled in his eyes. The old man clearly thought it was due to emotion over his offer.

"Good. It is settled then. We will now find the train station in this city."

He was still suspicious, but for now, had no choice but to follow. First, he had to get some opium for the journey.

They traveled for a full day, stopping at many small villages. Each time they stopped, vendors with food and drinks would swarm the platform, even getting on the train to sell to the passengers before jumping off just before it resumed its journey. The old man bought some food for him and his mother. He kept asking whether they had arrived in Bangalore, but each time the answer was no.

"They told me at the station that we have to travel on this train until we arrive in a place called Guntakal. There we will board a different one to Bangalore. You will see."

He hoped the old man was right and wondered if he had made the right decision to come with them. He only had a few more days of supply left for his mother.

They arrived in Guntakal the following evening. It was true; they all disembarked and were told to wait by the tracks for the train to Bangalore. He began breaking the opium nuggets in half, hoping he would have enough. After two days of waiting, he started to get nervous.

"Father, do you know if the train is really coming?"

"It was supposed to be here. I spoke to one of the porters. He said he heard from the station master there was a lot of fighting going on in Hyderabad. There are soldiers and a lot of killing. That is the reason everything is delayed."

"Hyderabad? But we left Hyderabad many weeks ago. How can it be that problems so far away are holding us up?"

"I asked the same thing. This is a different Hyderabad. It's not the same city we left in Pakistan."

"But why are there killings here? I thought we left all that behind."

"They are trying to get rid of the Muslims living there."

He didn't answer. But it seemed fitting to him that there was some justice in the reciprocity of their dislocation. After all, the Muslims did the same to us, he thought.

The train, when it finally arrived, was much smaller and narrower than the last one, and only had a few carriages. He noticed that the tracks only went in one direction, away from the station. But the crowds were the same. They had to push and squeeze their way on board to keep the family and all their bundles together.

All along the journey, he had been thinking whether he could steal one of the money pouches from this family. Yes, they had been kind to him, but he needed money, and they had plenty. His only worry was when they realized the money was gone, they would probably take him to the police. But if they couldn't find him in this new city of Bangalore, then maybe he could take the chance. He would have to wait for the right opportunity. Clearly, it wouldn't be while they were on the moving train. But perhaps after they arrived, there would be a chance in the chaos of disembarking. He would be patient.

The station in Bangalore was a very busy place. There were many tracks rolling in, and travelers everywhere. This was his chance.

"Father, you take the women off. I will follow you with the bundles. Don't worry."

The old man smiled at him, grateful not to have to carry any heavy loads.

He held back a bit as they all stood up and moved towards the exit of the carriage. He waited until the descending crowd had swallowed up the members of the family, his mother right in front. He knew where to look; he had watched the old man carefully during the journey to see which bundles he selected to get at his money pouches. There were at least three that he had seen, but he wasn't going to push his luck. One would do. And less likely to be noticed in the short term.

Slowly, he gathered up the parcels, gently lifting one of the money bags, and hid it in his dirty trousers. No one was paying attention to him. He made his way off the train and found the family waiting for him further down the platform.

"I am going to call a porter to take us to my niece. I think she lives in a place called Chamarajpet. You and your mother are welcome to come with us. I can pay you to work for me, and your mother can be comfortable."

The young man smiled, wondering if the old man had started to suspect his mother's addiction.

"Thank you, you are very kind. But we have taken advantage of your concern for us too much already. We have to start a new life here, my mother and I."

The old man smiled back at him. "I understand. You have been a very helpful traveling companion for us. But if you change your mind or need help, please come look for me in the Chamarajpet area."

The young man nodded and, without further ceremony, grabbed his mother's arm and moved off the platform. He wanted to get out of the station before they did.

CHAPTER 39

There was a lot of construction in Bangalore after independence, and the young man was able to find work as a day laborer. He and his mother had slowly put the harrowing events of their migration behind them, and he had eventually married. His wife was very young, but she took good care of his mother. He earned just enough money for them to rent a corner in a room in the northern slums of Bangalore. Normally his mother would sleep in the shelter, and he and his wife would sleep out front in the alley. It was only during the rainy season that all three of them would huddle on their side of the dwelling. His mother still needed her opium, but with steady work, he didn't have to resort to his old ways of theft to provide her with the drug. He found it easily in the drugs bazaar behind the KR market.

Over the course of their second year of marriage, his wife developed a terrible condition of acne. First, she would get red blisters along her cheeks and chin. Then, over several days, the blisters would grow into large pimples with big white tops. Her mother-in-law berated her even more than usual, as if the girl intentionally sprouted the volcanoes. The young man became so disgusted he couldn't stand to have sex with her anymore. Her face was rarely free and clear of the affliction, and she used a dirty piece of cloth to cover up.

"She is a leper," his mother finally told him. "We need to send her away."

"How do you know this?"

"I have seen the lepers in the place where they live. She looks just like them."

"What can we do about it? Shall we take her to the doctor?"

"You will waste your money. Don't you see, she keeps getting more and more of these disgusting boils? You need to send her away."

His mother was always too sure of herself. He looked at her, thinking it was probably the right thing to do, but wondered if there was an alternative. He never liked doing his mother's bidding. It annoyed him.

"Maybe I should take her to the medical shop. Maybe they have something that can cure her. There are so many new medicines now."

"I have never heard of this being cured. Anyway, you don't have enough money to buy anything for her. Just send her away."

He thought about this for a few days. He didn't want to give in to his mother too quickly. He thought he would take his wife to the medical shop rather than to the drugs bazaar. He preferred not to go to the same place where he bought his mother's opium. There was a very busy one in the train station. He passed it almost every day on his way to his job. There was always a long line of people waiting to buy medicines. It must be a good sign, he thought.

They set out late in the evening, after he had returned home from work. By the time they arrived, the owner had started to close the shop for the night. He ran up to Kumara, shouting at him to wait.

"What do you want? It's late, come back tomorrow."

"Hold on, I need you to see my wife."

"I don't need to see her. What is the matter?"

He pulled the shawl off his wife's head. Kumara took a step back from the horror of her face.

"She has been like this for a long time. I can't stand to look at her anymore. You need to do something."

"Wait here." He went back into his now darkened shop, looking for the new medicine he had bought just the other day. They had told him it was for pimples on the face. It came from Germany. A new miracle.

He counted out ten tablets. Would that be enough, he wondered. The girl's face was a mess. Best to sell him a few more.

"Here are some pills for your wife. She must take two every day. This is a very good drug. You are lucky. I just got it the other day for the first time. Ten rupees."

"Ten rupees? Are you crazy? That is a whole week's wages for me. What am I supposed to do?"

"My friend, this is not my problem. Do you want your wife to be cured, or are you going to stand here all night arguing with me?"

"I don't have so much money. You are a thief. You think I can't go somewhere else to buy this pill?"

"Try it. You won't find this one anywhere else but in my shop."

He took a threatening step toward Kumara, his fists clenched.

"I will give you one rupee today, and I will come tomorrow with another rupee."

"That's fine. I will give you two pills now and more when you come back. She will need many more before she is cured."

Grudgingly, the laborer came back to the shop at the end of every day to get more pills. After three days, he stormed back, complaining that nothing had happened and that his wife's face was still erupting.

"Are you crazy? She will need many more pills before she is cured. At least another twenty rupees worth before you will see any change."

"You are cheating me!" he shouted, pushing his finger into Kumara's chest. His mother had been right. He should have sent her away before going down this path.

"Don't you touch me, or I will call the police. Listen," he said, trying to calm things down. "You need to be patient. Your wife will get better, I assure you. This medicine is new. It comes from Europe. You will see."

The laborer was fuming, but he wasn't willing to give in to his mother. That was the only reason he bought two more pills before storming out of the shop.

Kumara shook his head as he closed up his shop for the night. All these foreign low-caste people were so different. They all felt entitled, somehow equal to their betters. He rolled his bicycle out to the road and headed home towards Cubbon Park.

CHAPTER 40

The next day Kumara went to the depot to get his inventory for the week. It used to be that restocking once a month was adequate, but in the last few years, everything sold out so quickly. He noticed a small, well-dressed man standing by the entrance of the warehouse. He had on a suit like the English, with a waistcoat and jacket. And even though he wore thick round glasses, he was squinting at the vats of liquids and boxes of pills.

"Greetings. Have you heard of the Pharmacy Commission?"

"No, I have not."

"Do you know about the Drugs Act of 1940?"

"Never heard of it."

"Well, I am giving you this written mandate from Delhi and the Drugs Commission. You must read it and be prepared to comply with the regulations in the next five years."

Kumara took the piece of paper that was handed to him. He stared at it, then handed it back to the man.

"Oh no, this is for you. It is your copy."

"But I can't read it."

"Ah, of course not. I will read it to you."

The man started to read the page, but Kumara couldn't understand a word.

"Are you reading English?"

"No, no, it is in Hindi."

"But I don't understand Hindi."

"Of course not, but after I read it to you, which is required, I will summarize for you in Kannada."

Kumara shrugged his shoulders and waited for the man to finish his gibberish recitation, which went on for almost five pages. By this time, four shopkeepers had queued up behind him.

"Now I will explain to you what this is. It is a new rule, imposed by the Drugs Commission and the Pharmacy Commission, requiring all dispensing of medicines to be licensed. This means that you will need to make an application to the Drugs Commission to receive a license that will allow you to legally sell the drugs. The application must be signed by a licensed pharmacist or a medical doctor, and you will have to pay the license fee, then you will receive your license."

The group that was now formed around the man was pushing forward, everyone trying to get closer to hear what the official was saying. One of them threw his hands open at his sides and asked in a very harsh voice, "But what if I am selling the drugs from a cart? I have a cart that I am moving around each day. Do I still need to have this license?"

"Yes, you do. There is a license for any type of sales, from a cart, a stall, a shop, a bicycle, a truck, anything used to store, transport, and sell the medicines."

The men shuffled around, uneasy at this proclamation. A different vendor asked, "But what did you say about the signature on the application? You mean it has to be a doctor?"

"Or a pharmacist."

"What is a pharmacist?" But Kumara knew what a pharmacist was. Geetha had explained it to him. He waited to hear the answer.

"An educated man who has studied the making and uses of medicines. He will have a diploma from a university with a registration number on it. You will need this number to make the application, as well as his signature."

"But I have never heard of this. Where do I go to find such a person?"

"That is your obligation. I cannot tell you. I don't know all the doctors and pharmacists in Bangalore."

One of the men shouted out, "There are only a few doctors in Bangalore. Don't you know this? We all have to go to the same doctor to get this signature?"

"Well, you have to swear that the medicines will be sold under the supervision of a licensed doctor or pharmacist. You must have them present in your shop."

"Are you mad?" another man called out. "Do you know how many shops there are in Bangalore all selling drugs? There are not enough doctors in all of Karnataka to do what you are saying."

The man blinked nervously behind his thick glasses. He clearly had not expected to be confronted and challenged by this group of ignorant merchants.

"Well, this is the rule. And shortly, many inspectors will be coming to see if you have all complied with the rules."

The men looked at each other, shaking their heads in disbelief.

"Where do we go to get this application that must be filled and signed?"

"You must go to the High Court in Bangalore and ask for the Drugs Commission office. There, they will give you the correct application for the type of merchant. When you have completed it, you must return it there, with the correct fee. Once the license is approved, it will be available at the Drugs Commission office until you return to get it."

Kumara didn't say a word throughout this exchange. He was trying to think how long it had been since Vivek had come to his shop to tell him that his application had been made. It was around the time his first son was born who was now almost four years old. That is a long time, he thought. Maybe it has been lost.

"Sir," he asked quietly, "do you know how long it will take to get the license once we pay the fee?"

"Oh well, it can take a long time. Every medicine shop in India has to do this, so you will have to wait."

"But if you will be sending inspectors to see our license, what if we have not yet received it?" another man in the group asked angrily.

"That will not be the case," the man quietly replied.

His audience was by now quite large, and with all the talking, shouting of questions, disbelief, and hand gestures, it was turning more into a mob than a group of men who were being lectured. The official was obviously getting quite nervous. He folded his Hindi proclamation sheet and eyed the exit of the warehouse.

As the official pushed his way through to leave, the conversation turned to the bribes they were routinely paying to the wholesalers.

"Well, I am not going to give another rupee to these thieves. I will just tell them that I am waiting for the license!" one of the group said, and everyone laughed.

A few of the wholesalers had also gathered around the

official to listen.

One of them, an older merchant from Calcutta called out to the group.

"You won't get away with that. I am taking a big risk selling drugs to you scum without licenses. If you don't pay, I will report you to the Drugs Commission and they will come and put you in prison."

No one believed him, and the proclamation they heard from the official that day was so muddy and confusing it was impossible to have a clear understanding of the state of affairs.

Only now, Kumara was much more interested in the status of his application.

CHAPTER 41

After Suresha had died some years ago, Kumara and his growing family moved in with Geetha in her two rooms near the Park. It was cramped, as Anu had delivered three more babies after his first son was born: two more boys and a girl. When he arrived home, he talked about the little man from Delhi who had come to the train station.

"Auntie, do you think that our license application has been lost? It has been a long time."

"Who knows…but there is no way to find out. All we can do is wait."

"Huh, wait until that horrible driver comes back to tell me the news. I have seen the car many times on the roads. Each time I see it, it reminds me of Vijay…"

Over the coming weeks, he forgot about the little man, and all the talk of licenses receded in his memory, replaced by the day-to-day chaos of running his shops.

One morning, he arrived at the station shop and found Vivek waiting for him.

"Your license has arrived," he said as he shoved a package at him. He turned quickly to leave, but Kumara stopped him.

"Hey, what am I supposed to do with it?"

"I don't know anything. Mr. Umesh just told me to bring it to you."

"Just wait a minute. I will have a look."

He opened the package and found in it only a single sheet of paper. It had an elaborate border printed in green, with encircled badges in each corner showing images of a snake climbing a cup. There were words in different-sized letters filling the middle of the page. Kumara impulsively smiled, very pleased with the grandeur and pomp of the document. He caught himself suddenly, not wanting to appear happy in front of Vivek.

"But there is only one page here. I have three stores. What do I do about the other two?"

The driver was irritated by the question. He didn't like these shopkeepers. But as he opened his mouth to berate him, he remembered the dead brother.

"Mr. Umesh knows you have three stores. This license is for all three," he made up. He just wanted to get out of there.

Kumara stared at him, knowing he wasn't going to get any more help from Mr. Umesh or his driver. He carefully put the license back into its envelope, and slowly, without saying a word, walked around Vivek to open the shop.

Anu and Geetha poured over the certificate that evening, both very impressed.

"Where are we going to keep this, Auntie? We have three shops, and I don't know if we have to hang it in the shop or keep it at home."

"This is very valuable. We must keep it somewhere safe."

"We can hide it under the mattress. No one will look for it there," Anu offered.

"For now I think that is a good idea. The next time I go to buy inventory, I will take it with me. When those thieves selling the drugs ask me for it, I will show it to them. Let's see what they say."

When the day arrived to restock the shops, Kumara carefully packed his license in its original envelope and carried it to the depot warehouse.

"I need to buy two bags of these pink pills."

"Do you have a license?" the bored attendant asked. This was the new routine. They asked for a license, then hit the buyer for a bribe when the answer was no.

"Yes, I have it here." This was not the expected answer, and the man was bounced out of his torpor.

"What? What do you mean, you have one?"

"Yes, I have one. It is here," and he took the colorful certificate out to show him. Several other buyers and sellers came around, fascinated by this turn of events.

"This is a fake. This is not a correct license."

"It is not a fake. It arrived from Delhi. See the symbols and the words. It is official."

The man studied the certificate. By now, a large group had gathered around Kumara.

"Wait here, I have to go check with my boss. Give it to me."

"You are not touching it. You can go bring your boss here. I am not giving it to you."

The men all jostled each other, trying to get a look at this mythical document.

"How did you get this?" one of the group called out.

"I made an application. You must have a doctor to help you." He had never internalized the distinction between a doctor and a pharmacist, no matter how many times Geetha had explained it.

There was a lot of mumbling among the crowd. Doctors were few and far in Bangalore. It didn't seem logical that they would each have to find a doctor to get a license.

"Did you have to pay a bribe?"

"No, of course not." He was enjoying being at the center of all this attention.

There was a lot of laughter and shouts of "I don't believe you!"

Finally, the attendant returned with his boss, who was visibly annoyed that he had been dragged from the comfort of his office to the dirty reality of his trade. They pushed their way through the crowd to the center, where Kumara stood waiting.

"Let me see this thing," he said, putting on his thick round glasses. The crowd went silent.

He examined the certificate that Kumara was holding up, looking at all the symbols. He then signaled his finger in a circle to look at the back. Slowly, he took his glasses off and replaced them in his shirt pocket.

"This is a correct license." The mob exploded into shouting and gesticulating.

"Ha, see," Kumara beamed at the crowd. "So I will no longer pay you a bribe to buy my inventory."

The boss hesitated before answering, trying to think of a reason to counter the assertion.

"Yes, yes that's fine," he grudgingly mumbled.

"Do I need to bring this with me every time I come to buy my product?"

"No no, I will just write the numbers from your license and keep it in my office."

Kumara couldn't wait to see Geetha to recount the events of the day. She had been right all along, and he returned home with the otherwise bribe he would have normally paid safe in his pocket. This was going to be a huge windfall for his family. All because of Vijay and Geetha.

Over the ensuing months and years, Umesh was approached by several matchmakers who had seen an opportunity in the imbalance between the demand for licenses required by the drug vendors and the scarcity of doctors and pharmacists available or willing to submit their qualifications for an application. The price to induce the holder of the diploma to assist in obtaining a pharmacy license increased dramatically. In fact, within a few years, Umesh had rented out his pharmacy license to well over a hundred medical stores.

CHAPTER 42

The young man's wife was finally pregnant, much to his mother's satisfaction. Her face still showed several scars from the blisters that had healed up, but she hadn't had any new outbreaks for some time. He was relieved that he didn't have to send his wife away, and there was a truce between him and his mother, albeit an uneasy one.

His wife though, was debilitated by the pregnancy. She couldn't keep a morsel of food down, which made her weak. His mother had a new reason to complain.

"This girl is vomiting all the time in our room. I try to send her outside, but she never makes it in time. I am always cleaning up after her. This is not my job."

"Do you think she is sick?"

"She is weak and sick. I told you to get rid of her."

"Maybe I should get her some medicine again. The first one worked so well on her face."

"You should stop spending so much money on her."

He glared at his mother, holding back the urge to slap her.

The next day he went back to see Kumara.

"Hey, my wife's face is much better from those pills you gave me. But now she is sick again."

Kumara was used to the non-specific nature of the descriptions his customers would come up with. He had learned to probe for symptoms.

"What is the matter with her?"

"Well, she is sleeping a lot, and she can't keep her food down. I am worried because she is pregnant."

"I have just the medicine for her—another new drug. You will see; it will help a lot."

After the usual arguments over price, he took a few of the pills home to his wife.

The shopkeeper had been right, it was a miracle. The very first day she took the pill, she was eating that same afternoon without any ill-effect.

"You see, the medicine worked. She has stopped vomiting."

"Yes, but now all she does is eat, eat, eat. We are spending a lot of money to feed her."

"You are never satisfied, old woman. Always complaining."

"And you are a fool to keep going back to that medical shop."

The baby was born mangled and disfigured. There were no arms, but he had tiny hands which extended directly from his shoulders. His head was very large, and his nose and mouth were indistinguishable from each other. The baby's eyes were permanently closed, and it looked like someone had colored his eyelids bright red with henna.

When he was finally allowed to see the baby, the young man was shocked and disgusted. He was sure this was a punishment from Shiva, but he couldn't think of anything bad he had done. It must be his mother, he thought, remembering his sister. She is evil. This is her fault, he was sure of it. But he was afraid to accuse her.

"This baby is a god and will bring us good fortune," his mother asserted.

"How can you say that? Look at it. It is a hideous monster!"

"You are ignorant and stupid. This baby is a Ganesha. You can see clearly here the trunk of the god growing from his face. You will see, this trunk will become longer as the baby grows."

"What about these tiny arms? Doesn't Ganesha have four arms? This baby doesn't even have any!"

"You will see, the arms will become longer and new ones will come from them. You will see."

"You should just take that thing and drown it in the lake," he said in disgust.

This prompted his wife to finally speak up.

"I won't let you. This is a precious baby, and your mother is right. We must care for it." She picked up the child and tried to get its twisted mouth onto her breast to feed it.

He slapped his wife across the face, infuriated by the alliance between the two women. She held the baby tightly as she fell to the ground.

"You are a foolish woman. This is a punishment, not a god!"

His mother stepped right up to him.

"Don't you touch her again. She is the mother of a god. This is a blessing to us, not a punishment!

He pushed his face up to her, fists clenched, desperate to punch her in the face. He turned and rushed out of the room. It was the only way he could stop himself from beating them both.

They shared their room with two young girls, a small boy, and their sick grandfather. The children scrounged enough money begging in the streets to pay for the shelter. They would each return at different times, first to see if the old man was still alive and then to give him some food and water before going back out. Whenever one of them came back to the room, the young man's mother would lift the baby and show him off.

"Look, look at this baby. It is a newborn Ganesha. Go and tell everyone that I will let them see the baby and they will be blessed if they bring money and food."

When the young man returned from work, he found the tiny room filled with people who had heard about the baby god. He pushed his way in and found his son lying in the middle of the room on a red and gold cloth, surrounded by flower garlands of yellow and orange. His wife was in the corner of the room, but his mother sat next to the baby, controlling the worshiper traffic, only allowing people to approach the child after they paid her with either rupees or food.

The procession continued through the night. The baby cried a lot. His wife tried to feed him several times, but it was very difficult. He would take a few drops of milk but then would cough and choke, and she would have to start all over again, trying to get her nipple into its twisted mouth.

"You should go to that medical shop and get some medicine so the baby will eat," his mother said, throwing a pile of coins at her son.

Kumara was surprised to see the laborer. He had hoped he'd seen the last of the volatile man.

"What is it now? Is your wife feeling better?"

"We have a son, but he is not drinking milk and crying a lot." The laborer was ashamed to share the truth about the baby's appearance and condition. "I need some medicine."

"I don't have anything for you. Just go." Kumara had learned to be careful about babies and medicine.

"I need medicine, do you hear me?" he shouted, grabbing Kumara's shoulders.

Normally his customers didn't get physical. He pushed the man's hands off.

"Calm down, I will give you something," he acquiesced. "This is a good medicine for babies. You have to give him one drop three times a day. It will help him sleep." It was the standard medicine for crying babies. He just wanted the man to leave.

The baby eventually fell silent. In three days he was dead.

The young man was relieved, but he couldn't resist accusing his mother of killing his baby.

"You wouldn't let the baby eat. You were so anxious to show him off and collect money. Your greed has killed my son."

"No, it was that criminal you got the medicine from that killed him, not me."

"The medicine helped him sleep. It didn't kill my baby," he shouted at her.

"You are wrong. The baby couldn't drink the milk. This is because of that medicine. You brought this misfortune on us," she growled at him. "At least because of me, we were able to get some money to compensate us for your mistake. Now we have to wait for another baby."

"I'm not touching her again," he came back at her vehemently.

"Ha, you'll see, you'll be sleeping with her by tomorrow."

The violence welled up in him, and this time, he struck his mother across the face. She turned back to him, blood coming out of her mouth.

"You are a fool. If you want to punish someone, go to that shopkeeper who sold you the poison. He is the one you should beat, not me," she spat at him. He pushed her hard. Coins scattered everywhere, falling out of her clenched fist as she fell into the corner of the room. His wife cowered against the wall, trying to keep out of the way. He grabbed some of the rupees from the ground and left.

CHAPTER 43

He wandered around for hours, seething over his mother's accusations. All she ever did was criticize and berate him. She was a bully. He was glad the baby died. It was an abomination. As he turned the events over in his mind though, reluctantly, he came to think that maybe the drops had killed the baby. That she might be right made him even more angry. Despite his attempts to stand up to his mother, he always ended up in this same place, acquiescing to her point of view.

He kicked a stray dog he passed on the road, needing a physical outlet for his building rage. His mother's challenge to him to avenge the baby's death slowly took hold and added fuel to his need for retaliation. As he passed through the market, he bought a small knife with the money his dead son had earned for him and headed toward the train station.

• • •

Kumara was having a very busy day. That morning, he had collected a lot of new inventory and was inside his shop at the station portioning out the pills and packets. Geetha was going to close the city stall shortly and come to manage the shop while he delivered the supplies on his bicycle. He kept having to leave the back room to serve the steady stream of customers interrupting his stocking, and this was making him very flustered and anxious.

Finally, Geetha arrived and this allowed him to finish up his sorting and packaging. He tied two huge bags of pills onto each one of his handlebars, fixed a box full of small vials and bottles onto the back of his seat with some string, and balanced a basket of soaps and other packets onto the front of the bike. He pushed off through the crowds on his way to the Russell Market. He would be gone most of the day.

Geetha was very good at her job, especially when it came to selling to women. She would size up each customer, deciding whether to flatter them and sell them lipstick or to cajole them into buying pills to cure their pimples, drink a potion to make their eyes brighter or color their hair.

"Look, this tablet will help you when you get a cold. If you are coughing a lot, you can take this so that you will feel better."

The girl at the counter had a red nose and was sniffling.

"You can buy three pills for a rupee. This should be enough. But if you don't feel better, come back and I will sell you some more."

The crowds always tended to thin out a bit in the afternoon. This was just the lull though, before the onslaught of the nighttime travelers and with them customers for the shop. She hoped her nephew would be back to take care of the evening traffic before it started.

A DANGEROUS TIME

When Kumara got to the Russell Market shop with his inventory, there was a line of people waiting. Anu was always overwhelmed by the crowds. She lacked confidence in dealing with customers and always ended up taking way too long to serve each one. He unloaded his inventory and stayed a bit to help her. This would make him late in returning to Geetha, as he had to go to the city stall before coming back to the station.

• • •

The young man was making his way slowly to his destination. Each step he took gave him more resolve to get back at the man responsible for all his troubles. He fingered the knife in his pocket lovingly, transferring all his anger and frustration into the one act he felt sure would regain his mother's approval and admiration.

He approached the stall and craned his neck to get a glimpse of Kumara. He could see a woman behind the counter, and he thought that perhaps his target was in the back. He pushed his way through the mob to get to the counter.

"Where is the man who is running this shop?" he asked brusquely.

"What man? There is no man. I am the owner. What do you want?"

The laborer was surprised by this response. How could this woman be the owner? Perhaps the man who had sold him the medicine was just a worker in the shop. But where was he?

"I want to see the man who was here before. He sold me poisonous drugs and my baby has died."

"Oh, you people are so ignorant. There is nothing in this shop that kills babies. You are a fool. Get out of my sight.

You can see I have real customers who are waiting to be served. Get out. Go!"

The crowd behind him was pushing and shouting at him to finish his business and let them through. The urgency and volume of their protests made the already jumpy man more belligerent. His eyes flashed at Geetha. This woman sounded just like his mother. With one quick motion, he drew the small dagger from his pocket and jumped over the barrier, grabbing her by the shoulder with his free hand. Jumbled memories of his baby, his sister, and the Muslims he had bludgeoned years ago gave him a kind of delirium. He drew her towards him and pushed the blade with all his strength into her belly. Surprised at how easily it went through her, he drew it out and stabbed her again and again. The mob on the other side of the counter exploded into shouts and cries. Some ran away, while others pressed closer to the bench to get a better look at what was going on.

Geetha fell to the ground. The young man kicked her, overtaken by adrenaline and a warm feeling of satisfaction. He kicked her again before climbing over the counter and pushing his way through the mob. A few of the men made a feeble attempt to hold onto his arms, but he shook them off and started to run. He ran very fast, looking back to see if anyone was chasing him. When he got out of the station he slowed down and disappeared into the sea of people congregating at the entrance.

• • •

Kumara closed up the city stall after putting all the supplies away and headed to the train station to finally relieve Geetha. He knew she was going to be cross with him for being late.

A DANGEROUS TIME

He came down from his bike and wheeled it toward the shop. He couldn't see Geetha, and no customers were standing in line. He was a bit puzzled. What was going on? He came right up to the counter and called out for her. There was no answer. He went around behind the shops to the door that led into the small storeroom at the back of his stall. He always brought his bicycle into the shop to make sure it wouldn't be stolen. He propped the bike against the wall. She was not in the backroom either. Bewildered, he looked out toward the front of the shop and saw her lying on the ground.

He rushed forward, kneeling down to help her. Suddenly, he noticed the blood. There was a lot of it, and her clothes were soaked. He lifted her head.

"Auntie, Auntie, wake up! I am here." Kumara cradled her head in his lap and picked up her limp hand. He stroked her hair which was untidy after the long day's work. He sat for a long time, waiting for her to move, to open her eyes. Finally, he accepted that she must be dead. He held onto his head and started to sob. He tried to get up, but his legs buckled under him. He thought he would go see the keeper of the stall next to his. They had been neighbors for many years and were quite friendly. But as he managed to stand, he saw the dark and quiet of the station, realizing that it was late, well past the busy time of the trains. The man would be gone.

Kumara rolled the metal cover down over the front of the store and went to find a porter. He was numb, moving in a daze. Being in the drug trade was not supposed to be dangerous. He couldn't fathom why anyone would target Geetha with such violence. She was so rarely at the shop. Maybe they were looking for me, he thought suddenly, a coldness coming over him, as if someone was squeezing the breath out of him. He had to stop and hold onto a wall on the side of the road to avoid falling.

Kumara arrived at the apartment with her body. When Anu saw Kumara at the door cradling Geetha, she assumed she was ill.

"What has happened Kumara? Did Auntie fall?"

"No, no, Anu. She is dead," he sobbed. He carried the body to the center of the room and laid it down gently.

"Dead? It's impossible. She can't be dead."

"Yes, I am sure she is dead. She has not spoken or moved for many hours. There is a lot of blood."

Anu let out a long shriek and fell backward. The baby started to cry while her other three children opened their sleepy eyes, wondering what was going on.

EPILOGUE

The area around the old fort in the original center of Bangalore is a busy place. Today, a huge bus station, medical buildings, and a dental school are the landmarks rather than the fort, which has almost disappeared from the landscape.

Forty years ago, it was different. If you made your way to this place from KR market, a quietness would emerge from the streets. You might see one or two wheelbarrow carts offering a few vegetables, t-shirts, shoes, and miscellaneous kitchen utensils. There is none of the bounty and color you would find in the bazaar.

Gangs of dogs roamed around, taking the place of tourists, children, and shoppers. As you moved behind the high street into the back alleys, you would see many unfinished one and two-story cement structures, without any cladding or paint, with gaping holes where the doors and windows should be. Each building would have steel rods popping from the roof in anticipation of the second and third floors, which never came. The city had forgotten this nucleus, forgotten why it all started here, as if it didn't even belong to the same geography.

The shop is tiny. It sits on the ground floor of a three-story building, but the other two floors are skeletons. There is a counter inside, but most of the goods are displayed outside the doorway. The owner sits on a dilapidated footstool. The first thing you notice is his withered arm. He is very thin and much better dressed than his surroundings, in an Under Armour t-shirt and a Yankees cap. It is hard to tell his age. His face is weathered and pockmarked, with a chilling scar across his cheek. It is the handiwork of a very angry customer from some years ago.

Inside the shop are homemade shelves crammed with every type of pill, ointment, salve, potion, toiletry, and dressing. There is no organization, no logic, no reason for the way things are laid out. Only the owner can lay his hands on exactly what the customer is looking for. Whether their ailment is real or imagined, everyone knows to come here for relief. He sells aspirin, codeine, steroids, belladonna, oxycodone, fentanyl lollipops, cannabis, laxatives, enemas, antiseptic creams, tea, candies and chocolate bars. A small cold box is stocked with beer, cola, Fanta, Orangina, and coffee drinks. There are plastic bags filled with dried leaves of every color and size and packets of condoms in streamers like lottery tickets.

He consults extensively with the occasional customer who visits him. Each transaction is conducted with great care and much discussion. It is not only his job to provide the remedy, but to ensure the return of the customer again and again.

On the few occasions when there is a prescription, he looks at it carefully, rubs his chin, asks a lot of questions, and then disappears into the shop. He times himself with his Timex watch, making sure to wait at least twenty minutes or more before reemerging with the required medicine. Another half hour is spent discussing when to take it, how to take it, with or without food, side effects, and, most importantly, when to return for more.

The shop served the city center for more than forty years. His father, uncle, and aunt, all long gone, ran it before him. His daughter attends pharmacy school, while his sons manage his other shops, giving him the chance to ease into retirement in this quiet, hardly busy stall. At the end of each day, he straightens the dilapidated frame that displays his faded and yellowed pharmacy license. He then brings all the merchandise inside, tidies up, and rolls the metal cover down over the front.

ACKNOWLEDGEMENTS

I would like to thank Dr. Mamta Sagar, an internationally acclaimed poet based in Bangalore, India, for all the guidance she provided on the cultural, societal and religious aspects of this book. Her input was invaluable, and helped bring the story to life.

My husband, Chris, read the book four times, and made important suggestions which made the book better. I hope to convince him to do the same for the next two books in the trilogy.

The book cover features the Maharajah Wodeyar's Rolls Royce Silver Ghost. The image is courtesy of Bonhams Cars Online.

My most sincere thanks and gratitude to all who contributed to this project.

Irina Simmons

Made in United States
Orlando, FL
07 March 2025

59249199R00166